Sue Gee is an acclaimed and established novelist. *Reading in Bed*, (2007) was a *Daily Mail* Book Club selection; *The Mysteries of Glass* (2005) was long listed for the Orange Prize for Fiction. She ran the MA Creative Writing Programme at Middlesex University from 2000-2008 and currently teaches at the Faber Academy. Sue Gee has also published many short stories, some of which have been broadcast on BBC Radio 4. She lives in London and Herefordshire.

Last Fling

SUE GEE

SALT

LONDON

PUBLISHED BY SALT PUBLISHING

Acre House, 11-15 William Road, London NW1 3ER United Kingdom

Printed in the UK by the CPI Antony Rowe, Chippenham

Typeset in Bembo 12 / 13.5

ISBN 978 1 907773 06 8 paperback

Salt Publishing Ltd gratefully acknowledges
the financial assistance of Arts Council England

1 3 5 7 9 8 6 4 2

For Jamie, the very best

Contents

In Bratislava

THE TRAIN TOOK all morning, and most of the afternoon, to roll through Czechoslovakia. He sat in a corner seat, his bag and briefcase up in the rack, the carriage empty. Silver birches lined the track; he looked out on to sunlit cornfields, red-roofed wooden churches, distant hills. Blue-nosed lorries from the fifties rumbled through villages; he saw stork, grazing in open fields; he saw a girl on a bicycle, riding down an avenue of shimmering poplars, her hair streaming behind her.

Sometimes he read; sometimes he stood in the corridor, feeling the rush of air on his face at the open window, feeling crowded Prague slip away. There was no buffet, there were few passengers — workmen got off at Brno, old women clambered on at country stations. Everyone visited Prague; few left the Czech Republic, crossing the border into Slovakia, newly independent, straining towards the future.

He went back into the carriage, opened his flask of coffee. Used to a crowded schedule of flights and conferences, he rarely had journeys like this. Ahead lay meetings in an unknown city: time now, in slow, unfolding hours, to consider his life, and what he might do with the rest of it, now everything had changed.

In the centre of the city, needing to change Czech to Slovak crowns, he found that the banks had closed. So,

late afternoon, had the bureau de change, and the girl in
the Cedok travel agency was unhelpful.

— Amex? she suggested with a shrug, and a glance at
his Liberty tie.

He nodded and felt for his wallet again, with its inter-
national credit cards, his company card, and the photo-
graph of Ella.

— Is not a problem. The girl was reaching for her bag
beneath the desk, her shift ending.

He nodded and walked out into the street again.
People were shopping after work, queuing for coffee and
cakes at the *kavernia*, waiting at tram stops. The bus from
the station had brought him past run-down post-war
estates, scrubby grass and balconies hung with washing;
here, walking along Jesenskeho Street, he reflected that
the queues were not as long as they had used to be in
Warsaw, or any of the Eastern European cities he had
visited, in a difficult market, before the Wall came down.
Now the market was opening everywhere, and here in
Bratislava he had appointments with directors from three
companies, anxious for foreign exchange.

His hotel, not far from the American Consulate, was
on the river front; he waited at the busy intersection by
the National Theatre for the lights to change. The light
was fading; the air had a wintry chill. He saw a couple
coming towards him, arms round one another, deep in
conversation. She stopped for a moment to push strands
of hair from her eyes; small earrings glinted; her lover
stopped with her, and tilted her face, smoothing the hair,
his mouth seeking hers, as people came and went.

He turned away, making for the glass and concrete
tower of the hotel.

His room was on the sixteenth floor. He opened the

window, looked out across the broad stretch of the
Danube, at the hideous suspension bridge slung across
it, the density of tower blocks beyond. He thought of
Prague, and bells, and tiled rooftops, domes and pinnacles.
He thought of London, of Ella, of turning his key in the
lock and calling out into the silence, dropping his bags and
frowning, calling again.

Clouds were gathering over the river. Street lights came
on. He kicked off his shoes and lay on the bed as the room
grew dark, his clothes still in his bag, tomorrow's papers
locked in the briefcase. Time enough. He closed his eyes
and the girl on the bicycle, fleetingly seen from the train,
came swimmingly towards him, became the lovely girl
in the street, drawn into a close embrace. He thought:
women for me now are glimpses, dreams. I have come to
a turning point: I must do nothing, and wait.

He sank into sleep.

The dining room was endless, half-empty, neon-lit.
Muzak played through enormous speakers. He ordered
a beer, and goulash, and looked through the papers for
tomorrow's meeting. Bratislava, once coronation city
for Hungarian kings, now refined crude oil, made pet-
rochemicals and plastics, pumped sulphuric acid into the
Danube. Tomorrow morning he would meet Jan Sloboda,
Ivan Kozia, Milos Razusovo, with whom he had corre-
sponded. Cheap labour, cheap chemicals, growing more
expensive as east met west. Cash in while we can, they'd
agreed in London.

Around him other men sat smoking and drinking,
reading the papers. He was used to this way of life, he
understood it, even though he had not expected to
become what he was: a buyer, a businessman, always on
the move. You came, you expected little, you were gone

in a couple of days. When you were home you thought about the next trip; travelling, you thought of home.

This is an empty marriage, wrote Ella, in the letter he had found on the kitchen table. He had loosened his tie; he read it standing up. Spotlights lit the humming fridge, the plants, her writing.

We have grown so far apart . . .

I no longer feel . . .

I have met someone who . . .

He poured a drink, fed the cat, read the letter again, frowning. The silence of the house stretched limitlessly away, then pressed upon him, as he himself had come and gone, leaving and returning. Trains and boats and planes and a book, a man living one life when he might have lived another: at home in a study, reading and writing and thinking, stopping for lunch with his wife, taking her to bed in the afternoons, having children.

He put down the letter, picked up the cat. She leapt away from him, made for the unlit upper floor.

Restless, unable to face his room or the bar, he walked along the waterfront, beneath trees, past the Slovak National Gallery, and nineteenth-century houses. Leaves blew about at his feet. He came to a sweep of road, leading left into the city—billboards, evening traffic, cafés closing. On the right, another bridge, with a footpath. He began to walk across, the air above the water soon even colder, and full of petrol fumes. Cars went past him; he turned and looked down.

Blue light danced in the racing oily water; a Dobermann chained on a piece of wasteland strained and barked up at him, guarding wrecked cars. A shrouded barge rocked in the wake of a riverboat, a half-moon hung in a hazy sky. How fast the river ran.

At length, the far side, a plaque on a wall. 1944. Built to commemorate the liberation of the city by the Red Army—with a few, guidebook words, it wasn't hard to work that out. Beyond the end of the bridge was only darkness: no street lamps, few houses, only another sweep of road, towards Vienna. He turned to look back at the city, saw the castle, high on a hill to the west. In Prague the castle was floodlit, magical. This was a box, a fortress, functional and implacable.

The cold from the river, the windswept bridge, the fumes, all made his eyes sting. He walked back, tasting something metallic, turning his collar up. The sunlit autumn journey had vanished, as if in a dream; crowded, familiar Prague and his house in London, which had been his home—they, too, felt immeasurably distant.

The morning was bright and cold. He went to the bank, took a tram to his first appointment, in a leafy suburb near the Slovak Parliament. The offices were furnished in sixties chrome and veneer; he was shown to a conference room and listened to a presentation in enthusiastic English, shown graphs and flow charts and prices of plastic granules.

Mr Sloboda was confident; along the table a bleached blonde woman in a suit snapped open a briefcase. His head ached, but he knew what he was doing: he smiled and signed the contract, and everyone shook hands. Clouds blew past the plate-glass window; two more meetings lay ahead. The smartly-dressed woman gave him her card; he slipped it into his wallet and thanked her, knowing he would not call.

He spent the rest of the day in meetings, lunching on a beer and sandwich. Back at the hotel, he showered, watched black and white television while he dressed. Government speeches, advertisements for non-stick pans and condoms. When he looked across to the window he saw that it had begun to snow—just a few fine flakes, but there, caught in the lights on the embankment, glistening far below, vanishing into the darkness of the river. It was the only beautiful thing he had seen since his arrival. He thought of the neon-lit dining room, with its muzak, and men alone; he sat in a plastic chair and dialled London, and Ella, and home. The phone rang and rang, and went on to voicemail; he hung up, took his coat and his book and went out, walking away from the river, and up towards the Old Town.

Beneath the flyover of the bridge, where traffic roared past the Cathedral, the last of the medieval city wall bordered the narrow streets. It was bitterly cold; snow shone on the cobbles. He found a square; he found a Hungarian restaurant, small and crowded and candlelit. As someone swung out of the door he smelt charcoal smoke, beer and spices; inside, the manageress at the till pointed him to a corner seat. Warmth, candlelight, a sizzling grill at the back.

— *Prosim?*

The waitress was young, with dark hair in a clip and eyes thick with black liner. He ordered a beer, fried potatoes and sausages; he spent the evening reading and watching her, as people talked around him. Now and then their eyes met, then he went back to his book. Snow fell past the window, it got late, the restaurant emptied.

The young man grilling meat at the back poured himself a beer and lit a cigarette. The waitress came over.

— Soon we are closing.

— Yes. He put down his book. — May I buy you a drink?

She hesitated.—Okay.

—A brandy?

—Okay.

He watched her go up to the bar, and reach for the bottle. Reflected light in the mirror touched her dark hair, her earrings. He thought: women for me are glimpses, dreams, but this is someone I could care for. He felt this instinctively, without knowing why.

She brought the drinks on a small metal tray. They sat opposite one another, the candle between them down to a stub. People hurried past the window, laughing in the snow. She waited for him to speak.

He asked her to tell him about her life. In formal English she told him she was studying law at the Komensky University, near the Old Bridge. He frowned: this must be Red Army Bridge, last night's place of desolation. Yes, she told him: it had been renamed in 1992. Of course, it was not so old, this bridge, but—she made a gesture; he understood. Everything had changed; new countries looked back for their sense of a future.

She was working in the vacations, hoping to travel abroad. No, she had never been to London. Her travelling had been mostly in Eastern Europe, though last year she had been for the first time to West Berlin.

And he?

He told her he had been travelling always, though this was his first visit to Slovakia, that he had not really planned this life—he turned the glass in his hand, watching the swirl of gold in the candlelight—but it was what he did, it was too late to change.

His family must miss him, she said, and he saw her glance at his ring.

He said:—My marriage is over, and gave a gesture, a

LAST FLING

shrug, turning away to watch the snow. — These things
happen, he said.
— There are children?
— No. He drank, imagining them. — Unfortunately
we—
There was a silence. The manageress, counting out
notes at the till, banged it shut. The young chef wiped
down the grill and hung up his knives. The smell of wine
and candles and charcoal hung in the air. They looked at
one another.
She said: — You were faithful to your wife?
— Always, he said, and it was true, though it had not
been enough.
— And now?
— Now it does not matter. He finished the brandy, put
down his glass. — And you? You are—
— I have no intention to marry. I must study for a
long time.
— Of course. Well — He drew a breath, feeling his
heart begin to hammer. — I must go.
She looked at him directly.
— Which is your hotel?

He lay on his back and she bestrode him, her unclipped
hair falling across her face, his face, falling through his
fingers as he reached for her, drawing her down towards
him, craving her mouth on his. Beyond her, at the uncur-
tained window, the snow was swirling through the night.
He felt himself drawn into a place at the heart of the
world, where everything began and ended; he closed his
eyes, came holding her blindly, and weeping.
Afterwards he held her tenderly, smoothing the thick
dark hair from her face, covering and stroking her, kissing
her forehead.

8

She said:—You are still in love with your wife, I think.

He could not answer her, he could not look.

In the morning the city was silent and dazzling. Grit was thrown down, but trams and trolleybuses moved slowly and few people were out. There was no traffic on the river. She told him she was going to walk home, to her apartment; the friend she shared with had gone to the mountains with her family; no one would have missed her. He pictured her climbing stone stairs, felt the cold of her empty rooms, thought of her making coffee on an electric ring, drinking it alone, with her law books on the table; sleeping before she went back to the restaurant tonight.

He held her close as they walked through the silent streets. He had one more meeting, at eleven. If the trains were running, he would go back to Prague; take the bus to the airport next morning, fly back to London.

And then?

—Let me buy you breakfast.

They drank scalding coffee, with slightly sour milk, in a *kavernia* on Tobrucka Street. There were rolls and jam, but no butter.

—Things are easier now, but still—She broke her roll in pieces, dunking it in the coffee.—Still we have a little way to go.

He watched her, pale and drawn but composed. All night they had been naked together. He reached for her hand.

—You are completely beautiful.

She drank her coffee, regarding him.

—Let me come home with you. We are just at the beginning. I can come back—

She shook her head.—These situations can be very

9

painful, I think. There are many things I want to do with my life. I do not want—She did not finish the sentence.

Out in the street he kissed her, folding her hands in his. Their faces were frozen.

—Thank you. You made me feel—He closed his eyes, drawn back at once into darkness and whiteness and she above him, a different woman, abandoned and entrancing.

Cold lips brushed his cheek.—We remember one another.

She walked away, not looking back.

He went to his meeting, then checked out of the hotel. The snow lay thick on the ground, but the trains were running. He sat in the restaurant car, lit all the way down by rose-coloured lamps, drinking and thinking as they pulled away.

Mother Duck

THE CALL CAME at nine in the morning.
  —I can't see the duck.
Snow was falling prettily. Hester, still in her dressing gown—it was Sunday—pulled on her clothes and went over at once, leaving her porridge uneaten. The trees, hedge and fencing along the back lane were trimmed with white; underfoot it was already crisp and even. Typical. Not a snowflake all Christmas, and now, in the middle of April—
  —*In his master's steps he trod*, she sang cheerily, as she rang the bell. — *Where the snow lay dinted*—
  Grace drew back the chain on the door and peered round it on her stick, hair all wild and age spots dark on her pale old cheeks.
  —It's nothing to sing about. She's completely disappeared.
  Hester followed her into the sitting room, radiant with snowy light. They gazed through the French windows, down the long garden, bordered with flowerbeds and ending in a dilapidated fence, smothered in honeysuckle. Beyond this was the main road, where the snow had quietened the usual endless traffic. In the bed on the left, Duck (Mallard) had for some time been nicely settled on a nest of this and that, twigs mostly, surrounded by daffodils and not far from the flowering currant. What a picture.
  —You see?

By now the snow was positively whirling. Duck and daffodils lay beneath a thick white coat.

—What are we going to do? She'll freeze to death. And the eggs!

Grace was trembling. She fumbled with the key.

—Here, let me. Is the shed unlocked?

—I hope not.

A few minutes later, hood up and fingers frozen, Hester had the spade out and was striding down the garden.

—Be careful! Mind her head!

—Don't worry!

—Hester positioned herself as accurately as she could remember—not far from the flowering currant—and began to scrape.

—Careful!

She dropped the spade and knelt down, sweeping the snow gently with her numbed fingers.

—Duck duck duck, where are you? she sang softly.

Grace was moaning from the step.

—There you are!

Bright of eye and calm as custard. What a clever bird. Sheep could survive in a snowdrift for days, but ducks?

—She's fine! She's absolutely fine.

—Get all the now off her, right off. We must make her a shelter.

—Go back inside, Grace, you'll catch your death. Go and look for something.

Ten minutes later, Duck was nestling beneath a snow-trimmed green plastic chair from the shed, neatly surrounded by kitchen trays.

—Safe and warm.

—Any chance of hot chocolate?

They had it half-listening to *The Archers*. In Ambridge

the sun was shining brightly, lambs in the background, talk of the Easter Egg Hunt.

—Oh, come on, Brian!

—She'll be fine now, said Grace, draining her cup.

—What a performance.

By the following morning, the snow was almost gone. Crystalline patches lay in the gardens, slush lined the pavements in the town. Hester, before she set out, rang Grace to check all was well.

—She's very happy, Grace reported. —I've had a peer.

—Do be careful, I'd hate you to slip. Do you want me to come and take it all down?

—Not yet. I think she likes it.

—I'll give you a ring after tea. Anything you need from the shops?

There wasn't: Grace was a stocker-upper, kept tinned steak-and-kidney pies under the bed in the spare room. You never knew. Hester pulled on her jacket, kissed the cat and set forth. Today was Daphne, who lived on fish-in-a-bag and needed the attic clearing.

—I want it done, she said last week. —It preys on my mind and I can't settle.

They had a preliminary look. Cardboard boxes tee-tered round a vast tin trunk, taken to India by Daphne's father in 1926; it said so, in faded letters on the front. A dressmaker's dummy stood nakedly in a corner; dusty stacks of pictures leaned against the wall: a mix of watery hill stations and views of the Himalayas, and fearful oils, done by a different hand.

—My great-aunt, said Daphne, now a great-aunt herself. —Do put them back, they depress me dreadfully.

—It's all quite tidy, said Hester, replacing a still-life

of bulging plums. She blew her dust-filled nose. — Quite organised. Are you sure you really want —

— Certain, said Daphne. — I need to know what's in those boxes. I need to get rid of most of it. I might have a lodger in time.

Hester, as they descended the stairs, with their dangerous frayed carpet, did not respond to this. Daphne had any number of rooms she could let if she chose, and a hairbrained idea every week. She told her she would start on Monday and charge £8 an hour.

— That's awfully steep, said Daphne.

— That is the going rate, said Hester firmly. She did not add Like it or lump it, though the words did come to mind. How did my life come to this, she asked herself, pulling up now at the gate, and knew the answer.

— It's all very well having a soft spot, her mother had told her, over and over again. — But you mustn't let people walk all over you, Hester. You must stand up for yourself.

A bit late now.

Daphne pressed a parking voucher into her hand the moment she came to the door.

— They're vicious. Vicious.

Hester stood scratching the card with her key as a warden came into view. She waved it at him brightly and slapped it down on the dashboard.

— Morning!

Then she went back up the path, wiping the last of the snow on the mat.

— Right, then, she said to Daphne. — I'll report at lunchtime.

Daphne was demanding; Grace a sweet anxious thing. Between them Hester's weeks might encompass any number of the ageing population, dotted along a radius from the centre of town to outlying farms, thatched cottages, bungalows with plastic windows, via rambling flats in Edwardian houses, whole Edwardian houses (Daphne) and the remnants of bedsit land. They weren't always female, her clients: she had a retired Lieutenant-Colonel and a retired headmaster; there was also Harold, the uncle of an old school friend, whose erstwhile occupation was not discussed. They did, however, all have one thing in common: they (like Hester) lived alone, whether through widowhood, divorce or (like Hester) lifelong singlehood, and none of them wanted, ever, to go into a home.

It was Hester who made possible their independent lives. She shopped, she cooked, she fed the cat, walked the dog and cleared the attic. She helped to choose the hat for a grandchild's wedding, and dug out a frock for the tea dance. She drove to the doctor, fetched the prescription and waited in Out-patients, patting a trembling hand and helping with the crossword. She changed library books, took on outings, picnics by the river; heaved out of the bath. This last had happened both with Felicity, eighty-one, clinging to the wreckage in her basement flat, and with the Lieutenant-Colonel, whom she had found beached like a whale when she let herself in to cook a lamb chop with new potatoes and runner beans, grown by her in her garden. She had any number of keys, all labelled and hung in her kitchen above the cat dish. She found the stopcock, cleared the drain. She built shelters for ducks.

— How is she? she asked Grace late that afternoon, phoning after a desperately needed pot of tea. Daphne's boxes had contained packaging from hairdryers, toasters, blenders, you name it, all kept just in case they needed returning to John Lewis. There were tarnished fish knives, pewter hip flasks, old twinsets, clouds of moths. A handsome microscope.

— That'll be worth a bob or two.

— It belonged to my uncle, Daphne said coldly. — I wouldn't dream —

There were some fifteen hundred curling family photographs, which Daphne wanted to sort and put in albums. Hester flat-packed all the cardboard for recycling, stuffed the twinsets in black bags and went out for mothballs. She drew the line, at least for today, at helping to sort the photographs, some of which went back to Paleolithic times, and briskly boxed up slithering heaps of negatives.

— Tomorrow is another day, she said firmly. — I'll be here at nine.

— How much did you say that microscope was worth?

The duck, Grace told her happily, was doing very well.

— Do come and see.

Hester went. By now the air was balmy with warm spring sunshine. They stood in the garden and looked down on it all, fresh and bright and snow-free, with its bizarre structure amongst the waving daffodils.

— Like a piece of Art, said Grace.

— Sort of.

Together they dismantled it, and the duck looked up at them respectfully.

— Or gratefully, said Grace. — It's hard to tell.

When everything was put away she poured two glasses of sherry and they sat on the patio drinking and munching Pringles.

— Another few days and we'll have a little flock of ducklings.

— And then what will we do?

—They can go on the pond. I'm sure that's what attracted her in the first place.

Hester said nothing. The pond was perhaps two feet in diameter, fringed charmingly with small rushes and kingcups, just in bloom. It was perfect for frogs. Not so good for ducks. Across the road was a large hotel, with a large garden, sloping down to the river. No doubt this was where Duck had come from. This was where she would, undoubtedly, want to return. Trouble ahead. But for now—

—Look! said Grace.—She's taking the air.

So she was. She waddled across the garden, taking little snips of this and that. She drank from the pond.

Hester and Grace were both filled with happiness, sipping their sherry as the sun went down.

She got home from Daphne's two days later to find a message on the answerphone.

—They've hatched! Grace's voice was quavering.—They're everywhere!

Hester was covered in dust. Her mind was full of the images Daphne had relentlessly thrust at her, over and over again: solemn groups of less-than-eminent Victorians, standing in front of potted ferns and studio backdrops; soulful portraits, newly engaged couples standing beneath monkey puzzle trees, endless games of tennis, table tennis, croquet. Then there were the travellers, posing before the Taj Mahal or the Pyramids, floating in the Dead Sea.

—That is Great-Uncle Stanley, said Daphne.—This is my mother's second cousin, Freddy Everett, whom I remember as a little girl. This is—now this is someone I can't quite place—

—I must go, said Hester.

The phone rang again, before she had time to respond

to Grace's message, never mind have tea, a bath, a bit of a rest, if that was all right with everyone.

—She's trying to get out! She must be wanting to get to the river, and they'll all be killed!

—I'm coming, said Hester.—Keep your hair on.

She picked up her keys, and fed the cat.

—I'll see you in however long it takes, she told him.—Don't wait up.

Grace was leaning on her stick at the open door.

—Quick!

They hurried through. Well, Grace couldn't exactly hurry.

—Steady on, said Hester.

They stood on the patio and surveyed the scene. Little flickers of life and anxious cheeping were everywhere, though at first Hester couldn't make it all out. Grace waved her stick.

—Look! There—and there—and by the pond—

—Where's Mother Duck? Oh, yes, I can see now.

Mother Duck was up at the fence, searching here and then there for a gap. One or two or possibly three of her brood darted behind her. Altogether there must be—

—At least twelve, said Grace.

—I'd say more. I'd say a hundred.

It was impossible to tell. No sooner had you counted one than it had darted away. Cheeping came from beneath the flowering currant, behind the compost heap.

Traffic was buzzing along the road beyond the fence. Mother Duck found a gap. Behind the smothering honeysuckle there were plenty. Within moments she was marshalling her brood. What a sight. What a parent. This was what the younger generation needed. Discipline. Purpose. Lining up: look at that. Quack quack, cheep cheep—

—No shilly-shallying, said Hester, in something of a trance.

—Do something! wailed Grace.

Hester sprang into action. Not for nothing had she been a Brownie. Not for nothing had she been a Guide. She still had the badges somewhere. One day, no doubt, she would be like Daphne, an Ancient Mariner, taking some poor helper through each and every one. But for now—

— Fear not! she told Grace. —Everything's under control.

Next Door had a gate. She ran round there, panted an explanation. Next Door, taking their tea, were thrilled.

—Where, where? Can we go and look?

—Just open the gate, said Hester.

They all rushed down the garden. Out on the road, Hester was just in time to see a yellow beak poke through Grace's decrepit fence, followed by a sleek brown head. The number 53 bus was thundering one way, a stream of four-wheel drives the other.

—Stop! commanded Hester, and stepped out into the road.

Everything screeched. There was shouting.

—Wait! she told them all, and held her arms out wide.

Out came Mother Duck, on to the pavement. Out came countless ducklings, all in a dear little row. Children in back seats shrieked and pointed. Every head was turned. Across the road, the Hotel Belle Vue stood magnificent in the April sun, its lawns sloping down to the gleaming river. Mother Duck, cool as a cucumber, stepped out past Hester's ropey old trainers and led her family towards it. Quack quack, cheep cheep. One, two, three, four . . .

Hester counted twelve, and then it was done. No, it wasn't. Just as she was about to wave the spellbound traffic onward, out came another one, all left behind and frantic. Poor little fellow—was it a fellow?—he'd never make it, all by himself. She bent down, and scooped him up.

Back

A T A TIME IN my life I prefer not to think about,
I used to make a bus journey each week across
London, travelling on the upper deck. I was living at the
time in the house of my friend Elizabeth, in an area of
the city close to one of the great parks.

Tall white terraced houses lay street upon street behind
the main road which ran past the park, and my memory
of those streets, which I had visited since childhood,
when they were rather different, shows sharp spring sunlight, bay trees in pots, dark ivy trailing over the walls of
secluded gardens. My memory of those days is in certain
respects unreliable, but I can see the delicatessen on the
corner where Elizabeth bought her cheese, and the dry
cleaners where American women quite unlike Elizabeth
or myself took their husbands' suits and shirts and their
own silken dresses, collecting them at the end of the day
in candy-striped paper bags. Women in pressed clothes
and narrow shoes, having a nice day now, while I went
to pieces. That is how I think of them, of it.

I unreliably remember sunlight: in fact, it was very
early spring, and often cold and sometimes raining, and
the journey I made on the top of that bus was through a
winter of the spirit.

Seasons are important; weather and houses are important; I dream about houses all the time. They are never

houses I know, but they must mean something. Elizabeth's house meant something.

Elizabeth had been at school with my mother. In the way that school friends sometimes do, they stayed in touch long after they had ceased to have anything real in common, and so it was that as a child I used sometimes to be taken for supper, and sometimes for Sunday lunch, to a tall dilapidated house quite unlike our own, in what was then a rather rundown area. Elizabeth was square and solid, with heavy dark hair and a strong, well-set face, and she lived with another woman, a painter called Louise. Naturally, when I was a child, the exact circumstances of their relationship were not revealed to me. I simply knew that there was Elizabeth, and there was Louise, who had a studio up at the top of the house where she painted, while Elizabeth went to work. She was also doing the house up, bit by bit.

I liked them both, and I liked the visits, going up dangerous front steps to the front door, squeezing past boxes of tools and paint tins in the hall, glimpsing a trestle table in the huge, unpapered sitting room. We went down narrow stairs to the kitchen, smelling fresh plaster and Sunday roast. A wall had been knocked down, floorboards had been taken up, unpainted glass doors led out to a small, neglected garden. Elizabeth was working on it, bit by bit.

She and Louise lived, it seemed, in harmony. I think I was always aware of their devotion, liking the way they walked round the garden together after lunch, Elizabeth's arm round Louise's shoulders as she talked about beds and plants and paving stones. I liked the way they looked at one another. Somewhere I was aware that my parents did not look at each other very much.

An only child, I was used to spending much time in the company of adults, or in my own company. When we went to supper, I would be put to bed in the dusty spare room, still with its original wallpaper, up on the landing across from the studio. I lay beneath a heavy paisley eiderdown, listening to the voices from downstairs. Next morning, I was allowed to sit in my nightgown on a high stool in the studio, watching Louise at work. She painted interiors, and views from the studio window; she painted Elizabeth, and once she painted me: we were both in an exhibition. I used to talk to her as I talked to Elizabeth: about everything, as children do. Then I grew older: I talked less and noticed more.

I noticed that the easy flow of conversation which Louise and Elizabeth shared, and which I had shared with each of them, was not something which went on at home between my parents: they were polite with one another. I noticed that the dilapidated house became, over the years, bit by cherished bit, a warm and well-ordered home. It made our house in Wimbledon feel too tidy, as if the furniture itself were being polite. Later, I realised that my parents' manner towards each other masked a deep disappointment and dislike. Later, they divorced. By this time, I had begun to think too much. By this time, Louise had died.

My mother moved to Edinburgh, where she had a cousin; she did not remarry. My father bought a flat in the Barbican; neither did he. Elizabeth and he had dinner from time to time; from time to time they went to concerts. Then these outings stopped. She was still in mourning; my father understood. He told me this one autumn Sunday afternoon, as we stood on the tiny balcony of his flat, looking down upon the lakeside terrace, where the fountains were.

I had not seen my father for months: by now I had my own adult life, which was proving difficult. I was too preoccupied with my own affairs to think of other people's. I was working, I was married: things were going wrong. I did not like the direction my thoughts were taking.

I told my father nothing of this. At the end of the afternoon we kissed goodbye, and I walked along the grey brick corridors past dozens of studio flats where people lived alone. I went down the spiral of concrete steps to the street by St Paul's, and caught the bus back to my own flat.

Then what had been difficult became intolerable.

My husband and I tried to make things better. We tried to have a baby, and found that we couldn't. Then he found someone who could.

It did not occur to me to go anywhere else. I rang the brass bell by the green front door and Elizabeth took me in. She made me a bed in the room of my childhood, next to her lover's old studio. I lay beneath the heavy paisley eiderdown beneath a painting of rooftops; I turned my face to the pillow and slept, waking in the small hours as usual.

I was off work; I was given pills; I was going to pieces. So. This journey. I came out of Elizabeth's front door and down the steps; I walked through those white streets and up to the main road, crossing to the bus stop when the lights changed. People were still in their winter coats. Mine was absolutely straight and black, long, beautifully cut: the last thing my husband had bought for me. Clothes are important, too: when I am well, I notice everything.

People queued, shivering; they hurried through the

park and took refuge in restaurants. The bus came; I climbed to the top, wanting to be above the press of traffic; I sat at the front, looking out, seeing nothing. I truly can remember nothing, until we drew near to my destination.

A four-lane road, a roundabout. White road signs hung just above the level of the upper deck. Miles and fractions of miles — to the river, the railway station, to the East End — passed above my head. We moved into the far left lane. I did notice now: I noticed everything. Racing heart, tight chest, empty stomach churning. An enormous Victorian building engrimed with dirt, rust on every metal window frame. Litter blew in the wind; pale young women pushed babies in plastic shrouds. If the sun ever shone, I do not remember it. I remember the dusty windows of the bus and a leaden sky above the roof of the hospital. I remember my appointment card, a pale spring green, and a list of dates and dates and dates.

Dr Morgan had private consulting rooms in a street in the heart of the city: I could not afford to see him there. I pictured the discreet closing of a heavy polished door, leather chairs, glossy magazines. Here, I sat not in a waiting room but a waiting area, a space. A girl at a desk had a computer screen before her; a large box of toys stood on the floor for those who had come with children.

I had no children.

Each week, I had thirty minutes with Dr Morgan. I entered his little room and sat down; the black coat, unbuttoned, fell away to the sides of the low chair opposite his; on the table between us was a box of tissues. Once, as I talked, I remembered a woman sitting before the long illuminated mirror of a very expensive hairdressers I used to go to in the days when my husband loved me. The woman was a few seats along from me: I became aware of disturbance. I turned, I saw her weeping, her hands and her long wet hair covering what I could see, when at last she looked up, was a fine and lovely face. Scissors stopped, coffee was brought, Lenny was all concern. Cheer up, he told her, no man is worth it. I saw her fail to smile.

Why are you telling me this? asked Dr Morgan. What is that woman to you.

I liked her, I told him, and I knew why she was crying. She had been trying not to cry for years.

Have you been trying not to cry for years?

Perhaps. Probably. Yes.

About—

Everything everything everything—

Then it was time to go.

I climbed the steps of the house of my friend Elizabeth and unlocked the green front door. It was starting to rain, it was after four. Elizabeth was still at work. I was still off work. A letter lay on the mat: I picked it up and went through to the hall, with its paintings by Louise and faded blue and ochre rugs, and down the stairs to the kitchen.

A bowl of hyacinths stood on the table and the air was full of them. I put on the light above the cooker; I propped Elizabeth's letter up against the hyacinth bowl, I put on the kettle and greeted the cat as he came in through the cat flap. He left blurry wet pawmarks on his way to the fridge; I fed him, and stood at the glass doors to the garden as the kettle came softly to life behind me. I watched the rain fall on to the paving, mossy here and there in the cracks; it fell on to clay pots of bulbs, still tightly in bud, on to variegated ivy and leafless shrubs. A dark walled garden, just the right size; a little stone statue: a girl, an urn.

The kettle boiled. I made tea in Elizabeth's blue and white pot and sat at the table and drank it. Rain trickled down the glass doors, the heating came on with a leap like a cat; the cat, beneath a radiator, washed and washed. Above us the house was absolutely quiet.

Rain falling as darkness fell; an empty house; a marriage ended.

I put my head on my arms on the table and waited for Elizabeth to come home.

I woke to see her standing on the other side of the kitchen, reading the letter. She had switched on the low lights above the worktop and for a moment, still half-asleep, I saw on her well-set face an expression I had never seen before: closed, clouded. Then she put the letter in her pocket, came across and sat down opposite me: she smiled, and her face was as it usually was.

—All right?

—All right. I touched the cold teapot. —I'll make us some more.

—No—let's have a drink.

We opened a bottle of red and she drew the curtains. She asked me, as usual, about my day. I told her, as usual, that there was little to tell. She described her own: I sensed it was somehow an effort. We sat listening to the rain; she refilled our glasses. I wasn't supposed to drink with the pills.

—What shall we have for supper?

I shook my head. —I'm not hungry.

It was what I said almost every evening: I waited for the usual kindly coaxing. She said, in a tone which was flat and weary:

—Please—

She looked suddenly tired—more than tired, exhausted;

and watching her I saw again the fleeting expression I'd glimpsed earlier pass across the features which her lover had painted so often: such a strong, beautiful face. Now it was not just tired but older, much older, aged between morning and evening.

I thought: she's had enough of me, she can't be doing with all this any more, I shall have to go—

Panic began to rise in me, I got up quickly, turning away, turning on the radio, hearing myself say in a high, faraway voice—

—It's all right, I'm sorry, I'll get supper, you must be—

Bach was on the radio, I do remember that: a harpsichord, I do most clearly remember, repeating a theme which ran over the keyboard up and down up and down up and down, relentless and cruel, as if the containment of passion were something so simple and plain.

—Jo—

Behind me, a hundred miles across the room, Elizabeth was getting to her feet. I opened the door of the fridge and could not recognise how to put one thing with another. I took out the box of eggs and put them on the worktop beside me, I swung the door shut, shaking; I put my head against the cool fridge door and tried to breathe. I thought: there are pills and pills and pills upstairs, I shall swallow the lot and they will save me—

—Jo?

I could not look at her.

—I'm sorry, I said to the egg box.—I'm sorry, I'm sorry, I'll go, it isn't fair on you—

—Darling, said Elizabeth.—It isn't you. It isn't you, it's me.

—What?

The harpsichord had finished, and now there was a play.

—Come and sit down. Please?

I switched off the play and sat down: I looked at her. Not just older, but thinner—she had grown thinner: how had I not noticed that? What else had I not noticed?

—What is it?

She picked up the letter. I'm sure she would rather have told anyone but me, but she had to tell someone, and I was there.

Next morning, when I woke up, things were rather different.

I got out of the bed with the paisley eiderdown, in the house where I had spent some of the nicest days of my childhood; I put on my dressing gown and went down stairs and made us both tea. I took the tray to Elizabeth's room and drew back the curtains and kissed her. She was already awake, and the cat was sleeping beside her. We drank our tea together, and then I left her, and went downstairs and made a telephone call. And then that part of my life was over.

I am sitting at a table on the terrace at the Barbican. It is mid-morning, midsummer, a Saturday. Ducks drift over the green-black water of the lake, between the fountains; the church clock strikes on the other side. People come and go, in no hurry, enjoying the sunshine; they push open the heavy glass doors, carrying trays of coffee and pastries, and as they do so phrases of a string quartet in the foyer float out, and are shut in again. I think they are playing Bach, but it does not sound as it sounded on the radio that terrible evening—relentless, merciless. It sounds okay. I stir black coffee in a white cup, look at the paper and wait for my companions.

The church clock strikes the quarter hour: I look up. Families are feeding the ducks, restraining toddlers at the water's edge. At the far end of the terrace a couple are walking slowly, arm in arm: he tall, with a bit of a stoop, grey-haired, wearing glasses; she shorter, thin in a way anyone can see is not natural—the way her clothes hang loose, the original square shape beneath them clearly needing more flesh to fulfil itself. She wears a straw hat, dark glasses, leans on him.

They are looking around: I rise to greet them, I wave—to my father, who raises his hand, to Elizabeth, who smiles. I pull out chairs for them as they draw near; we kiss, and Elizabeth slowly sits down.

—More coffee? asks my father, seeing my empty cup.—I'll get it.

Elizabeth and I sit next to each other, watching him go. She will have tea—coffee does not agree with her now. There are quite a lot of things which do not agree with her: with her illness, her thinness, her skin beginning to draw tight across her face.

In spite of all this, she is more beautiful than I ever remember.

—How are you? I ask her.—How did you sleep?

—I'm tired but I can't sleep, she says.—It's a bloody nuisance. Never mind.

I put my arm round her; she leans against me, watching the glass doors. We wait for my father to rejoin us.

There are people excluded from this little company we make. My mother, walking her dog in Edinburgh, writing me brisk letters. My one-time husband, with his new wife, new baby. My one-time self: restless, anguished, making a bus journey across the city so that I could cry, counting up stored-up pills.

She's gone.

I stepped back from the brink.

Sitting there now, my arm round Elizabeth's thin shoulders, I think about marriages, which sometimes work and often, if the truth be told, do not. I think about Elizabeth and Louise, who loved each other always, and I think about friendship, which seems, in my present state of mind, to be the thing to aim for.

Then my father comes out through the glass doors, making his way towards us. We sit with our drinks in the sun, watching the ducks, the children, the rise and fall of the fountains, seeing Elizabeth through.

Landscape at Iden

H UGO WAS CONSUMING a pear. Alone in the pan-
elled dining room, he spread his napkin, peeled the
freckled yellow skin with an ivory-handled fruit knife,
quartered the juicy white flesh. Sun gleamed here and
there, striking the rim of a glass, a silver blade, the fruit
dish. This, in the afternoons, was the darkest room in
a house positioned for darkness: sunk below a towering
bank at the back, the long lawn up there bordered by
conifers. He had bought it when he had money, soon
after the war when large country properties like this were
cheap, people struggling with death duties. No one else
wanted to live there, no servant would come there: all
that way out in the middle of nowhere, all those rooms
to clean. When the agent showed it, unlocking the door
to the huge hall, putting back the shutters, it had been
empty for months.

He and Phyllida had been married just over a year.
They climbed the great staircase, looked out of the
master bedroom on to the drive, curving round uncut
grass; scanned the tree-lined road, the glimpse of ditch
and cornfield. They went into other bedrooms, while
the agent looked for the stopcock; he came back, and
ran rusty water into the ancient bath. Pipes banged and
shook. They went down the back stairs, into the kitchen,
where beetles scurried away beneath the vast black range.
Outside, they climbed the flag-stoned steps up the bank,

walked over the lawn. The autumn sun came out and the conifers cast dramatic shadows. Behind this levelled stretch the ground rose again, became a wooded hillside.

They looked down on the house, so spacious and forbidding, and knew they would live there. Phyllida was young, just out of the Slade, and full of energy. Hugo, rather older, had his inheritance. He had survived the war, and he knew how to invest: this would be their grand project. He made his offer on the fourteenth of October, 1919, and had it accepted at once. When the girls arrived, the house was filled with life, with calling voices. It was full of them still, all these years later: he was surrounded by women, calling mostly to each other.

Late September, Sunday afternoon, an Indian summer. Outside, the heat was intense, the air full of butterflies, dragonflies, bees. In here, such cool, such shady quiet. Hugo finished the pear, his second, picked yesterday from the espaliered tree on the kitchen garden wall; his elbows rested on polished mahogany. He had noted Phyllida's sigh as she rose from the table, leaving china, silver, crumpled linen, glasses with a residue of wine, all for him to clear. Too much eating, too much sitting about: her unspoken rebuke, as she swept the girls out with her. They patted him vaguely as they passed, dropped a kiss on his balding head.

—Dear Daddy.

—We'll come and help you later.

A fly buzzed in through one of the tall casement windows, open to the front.

His geese were out there, asleep beneath the trees. Later he would go out with the bucket. Later he would clear the table. It was Sunday, there was plenty of time. He watched the fly, and reached for the jar of biscuits. Sleepy, sleepy Somerset. Up on the back lawn, Phyllida had her easel out, stood obstinately before it in her sunhat, surveying mellow chimney stack and lichened tiles.

There had once been talk of doves — Think how lovely they'd look on the roof, said Hugo, but this, like so many things, had never happened. — We can do anything we want, he said, but of course they couldn't. He was given a snow-white goose and a gander: they bred, and he was happy. — Everything I want is here, he said. — You, the house, the girls — don't you feel that, my darling? Phyllida?

Madeleine had dropped her sandals on the step by the back door: they were just visible from up here, unfastened from slender hot feet as she went indoors for a drink. Bare feet on a tiled floor: what bliss. A scattering of geranium petals lay on the flags, brushed off in Phyllida's early morning watering of the pots, filling the tall grey can from the water butt. Down there, the darkness of the house was a refuge; up here on the baking lawn her hair clung to her head beneath the straw and a bead of sweat was trickling down her neck. She wiped it away, wiped a streak of burnt sienna on her shirt: the oils were almost melting. The painting had been troubling her for weeks; this meant her whole life was troubled. Should she flatten, foreshorten, dramatise? She wanted the plunge into darkness, the sunlit roof and dazzling grass above, and then the blank black windows on the façade, the fall into shadow, deep and endless. It was difficult, difficult. She could not get it right, could not decide.

A dragonfly darted in the air before her, was gone with a shimmer of wings. Bees sailed in and out of Hugo's hive.

— I will not be distracted, she said aloud, and dipped her brush.

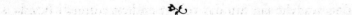

The girls were upstairs, in Madeleine's bedroom. The curtains were drawn against the heat, across the open window; everything was shadowy and soft. Heaps of clothes lay on the bed—what to wear, what to wear? They had been trying on all morning—not that there was anywhere to wear a shred of it. In two days they would be back at school, Maddie in her last year, Florence with two long years to go. Ahead lay months of awful meals, double maths, deadly history, church, and Sunday walks in pairs.

—I survived it, said Phyllida, whose school it had been.—I even enjoyed some of it. What did she know? It hadn't mattered about the School Certificate for her: she knew she was going to be a painter, had left and gone up to London—at Maddie's age! She talked about it still: the Antiques Room, the Life Class, the Summer Exhibition; the parties, the picnics, the dancing on the grass. London, London! Everything had happened there, everything was fun and alive.

—And then she met Daddy, said Flo, holding up a silky camisole, the colour of *café au lait*.—And then they came here. Where nothing ever, ever happens. Why? Why did they do it?

—You know why, said Madeleine, all older sister, yawning after all that lunch.—It was a sort of vision, wasn't it, something dramatic. Things like that only happen once.

Her school trunk stood in the corner with the lid up. They had been into town with their mother and bought new shoes and gymslips; everything was washed and ironed and mended now; she had done almost all her packing.

—I haven't started, said Flo, dropping the camisole. This was the last Sunday of the endless summer holidays. Everything was endless: the holidays, the term; she was waiting and waiting for things to begin. Here were all these lovely clothes from her mother's day, here they were dressing up like babies, playing at it all, with not a party to go to, not one ounce of glamour or excitement, only the dusty road, the echoing house, her parents.

Had she always felt like this?

— Why did they get married? she demanded, picking up an indigo blue kimono.

— Stop it, said Madeleine, winding a turban round her head. — You know why. Daddy fell in love. He walked into a gallery after the war and saw her in a crowd of people and knew she was the one. Just as they knew about moving here. Why do you keep asking? Of course — she tucked in the ends of *eau-de-nil* silk — of course she loved him too.

— They hardly talk, said Florence, slipping into the kimono. — And we're all just stuck here. She walked over to the long dim looking-glass. Those white and crimson water lilies embroidered on the blue, that square-cut sleeve — she held up her arm and watched it fall away. Should she let it all lie open, or tie it at the waist with satin ribbon?

— I love this house, said Madeleine.

When this baby is born, when this baby is walking, when the dining room is finished, when this painting is done — then I shall be happy. Thus had time passed for Phyllida.

Had she always been like this? She couldn't remember, knew only that life, always, lay in the future. Even when she was painting, doing what satisfied her as nothing else, it was always, When I get this right; it was always a struggle. So of course, when she was young, and had seen the house on that autumn afternoon, life seemed to beckon as never before. All that emptiness, waiting to be filled. All that neglected grandeur, waiting to be restored. London, where she had met her new, improbable husband, faded like a dream. She was a fragment there, a mote in a swirling shaft of dust. Here—she could claim, she could conquer. Happiness was only waiting: soon she would be there.

And now—oh, now! If she put this canvas away, stacked it up in the studio with all the others, abandoned the whole idea and started again—then she would do it all quite differently. If she were Nash, if she were Nicholson—she had seen their work in London, in the spring, the catalogue was in the drawing room—she would cut to the bone, cut out every detail. Geraniums! Lichen! What nonsense. She needed only the drama of design: the slope of a roof, the dizzying perspective, that long dark fall. Or perhaps she should think still more boldly—about the strangeness of building a house here at all, against a towering bank, with no other house for miles on either side. Strangeness: that was the key to being modern. If she were Paul Nash she would place the house in the cornfield across the way—adrift, alone, mysterious, with the bank closing in behind it. Or he would take the flight of steps and place it in the lane: there, without reason, stretching to the sky. You would look at it and feel unsettled; you would look at it and wonder about its meaning, and something in you would be moved, without you knowing why.

That was what she had felt in the spring, up in a London gallery again and gazing at an endless shoreline made of planes of muted colour; at a window frame floating over a winter garden, an autumn landscape so still it felt as if time had stopped for ever. *Landscape at Iden*: a stack of logs, a trug, a screen; the shadow cast by a single pole;

a field beyond studded with angular bare trees; a distant
gate to hills, motionless clouds. Muted ochres and greys
and then that strip of blue, those watchful clouds. No
one could explain it: why the screen was there, why the
pole, how that shadow was cast in a sunless place. Why a
serpent coiled along the fence. And no one could explain
why that conjunction of objects, that stretch of land, could
pierce you with an ache of longing and recognition.

Why had she ever thought she had something to say?

Better to stop, stop now, and face the truth.

—But if I don't paint I shall die, she said aloud, and
then, in an access of self-loathing, flung down her brush
on the grass.

Hugo, doing the dishes in the shady kitchen, heard her
cry, looked up but could not see her. Then he did: she was
striding across the lawn in a fury, closer now to the edge
of the bank, the top of the long flight of steps. Would she
come down? Would she let him soothe her? She strode
past: a streak of cotton smock and yellow sunhat and she
was gone. He gave up: no, he must never give up. And
he lifted a Doulton plate—the last of his grandparents'
dinner service—and put it, dripping, into the rack.

He washed up everything, china and silver, and glass
in a fresh bowl of water, setting the glasses to dry on
a worn old tea towel, catching the glints of light from
the sun which was sinking slowly, over the wooded hill
beyond the bank. The house faced east-west, in summer
the best possible position: with the bedrooms at the front
you woke to sunrise, breakfasted in good morning light,
the perfect start to the day. You gardened and saw to
things up at the back in coolness, shadow and dew; in the
heat of the afternoon you read and rested—or painted,
if you were Phyllida; as the sun moved slowly round,

you lit the drawing room fire. He lit one every evening, even in summer, marking the transition between day and evening as it should be marked: with a drink, with brightness before the dark.

Life was simple here, simplicity and routine the key to happiness. And though he was no artist he loved beauty above everything: loved the glint on those glasses (he dried his hands); the dull gleam of old gold picture frames in the passage down to the drawing room; Phyllida's paintings, hung all along the corridors and in almost every room—how good she was, if only she could see it. That portrait of the girls; the cat, sleeping all afternoon. How well she had done the house—the curtains and bedspreads from Liberty sales, his family furniture settling in so well, everything belonging together. Of course, he had had money. The truth was he had less money now. School fees and running the place and living on interest without adding to capital, half shrunk away in the slump: it all went before you knew it. Still—everything was done and settled, not a teaspoon needed, and even if war came they would be safe down here. Thank God he was too old for service now. They could live out of the kitchen garden if they had to, pot rabbits if they had to. Nothing like rabbit stew.

He went to the open back door and looked up the dark bank.

—Phyllida?

No answer.

He'd leave her to it, calm her down later with tea. Time she had a show again, give London a try: he'd suggest it. And he stood there in the shadow, listening to the afternoon: the droning bees, his geese at the front, stirring themselves as the day grew cooler. Time they were fed and watered. He picked up the bucket, filled it from the tap on the waterbutt—this, too, he loved, that rush of water, the sight and sound of it—and carried it round the side, hearing now, from deep within the house, the gramophone start up. The girls must be down, playing—'Smoke Gets in Your Eyes' for the millionth time. Did they never tire of it? And he took the bucket round to the front and the good old geese got to their feet beneath the trees and greeted him.

Madeleine, in the turban, Florence in the kimono, were flung out across the drawing room sofa, singing languorously along. It was much cooler down here than up in the bedrooms and Flo's mood had softened.

— *They asked me how I knew my true love was true . . .*

You weren't supposed to like the sound of your own voice, but she couldn't help it.

Perhaps one day a man would come quietly up behind her as she sang and stand listening there until she turned around, and jumped, like the people in *Private Lives*, which Maddie had seen and told her all about.

— *Some day I'll find you, moonlight behind you, all of our dreams will come true . . .*

— You always had a very sweet voice, Miranda.

Perhaps she could change her name.

Madeleine lay on the cushions, drinking everything in: the last of the roses, dropping dusky petals on to the window table; the funny old screen, which had been her grandmother's, all Victorian decoupage and yellowing varnish; the portrait of her and Flo which her mother had done when they were little and which Daddy always said was his favourite thing in the house. In two days' time they'd be travelling back to school, where everything was plain and hearty. She would try to hold on to all the things she loved. The room smelled of ash from last night's fire;

dusty sunlight filtered through the window; the gramophone record hissed and sighed, and the singer sounded a hundred miles away.

—*I of course replied,*
Something deep inside cannot be denied . . .

Would she, could she, ever feel like that? Would she walk into a gallery, as her father had done, back from the war and lonely, that was how she imagined it, and see someone walking through the crowd, looking at pictures as he liked to look at them, holding a glass in his hand and turning, catching her eye? Would they know straight away it was real?

The record was winding horribly down, and the singer began to sound as if he was dying, all deep and strangled.

—Put it on again.

—You do it.

But Flo would not move.

—I'm in a trance, she said.

Hugo, returning with the bucket, heard the strains of the song floating out once more.

— *They asked me how I knew my true love was true . . .*

Though the girls had been playing the song off and on all summer, though he knew it by heart, he stood listening now with sudden aching sadness. Not good to keep thinking about the past—that beautiful, golden, filigree of the past—he knew it; most of his thoughts were not worth having anyway, he knew that, too. Hold on to now, be glad of the moment, that was the way to stay steady. But the moment—this moment—was not as it should be, a slow and contented summer afternoon. In two days' time the girls would be gone, and then how empty the place would feel again.

Where had Phyllida gone off to?

How had he ever thought he could keep her happy?

He set down the bucket by the waterbutt and stood looking up at the bank. If he went up and found her returned to the easel he would only interrupt her; yet he needed to know she was back from wherever she'd gone, just needed to know she was here.

— *When a beautiful thing dies, smoke gets in your eyes . . .*

Surely, for once, they could play something else. He went back into the house, walked down over the worn rugs in the corridor and opened the drawing room door.

There they were, singing like angels, all dressed up again, draped across the sofa like something out of Leighton. Light of his life.

—Hello, my darlings.

—Oh. Hello, Daddy.

They opened their eyes and gazed at him from some faraway place.

—Have you done the washing up?

—We were going to help you.

—Never mind.

—Where's Mummy?

—Gone for a walk. I expect she'll be back soon.

The record was winding down again, all those long vowels getting longer and longer until the whole thing became a joke.

—Could you put it on again, Daddy? As you're there.

—What about something else?

And he walked over to the table and looked through the pile of records in their brown paper sleeves.

—What about this?

He slipped it out, Phyllida's favourite. Perhaps if she heard it, returning, it would change her mood.

— *In the wilderness build me a nest, and remain there, for ever at rest . . .*

But as soon as he heard it he knew he was wrong, and how had he not seen it before? This song was not about returning, but leaving for ever, and why should it bring her back to him? What would ever do that?

—Daddy? What are you thinking about?

—Nothing, he said, as he said so often.—Time for tea.

—He's so *ordinary*, said Florence, when he had gone.

Phyllida came back; they had tea on the lawn. The girls took off their dressing-up things and carried up the tray and the cake; he followed with the scalding teapot. The easel had been turned away, and stood facing the wood on the hill. The table was in the shade of the conifers, but even so—

—It's so hot.

—Where did you go for your walk, Mummy?

—Just along the wood. She took off her sunhat and fanned her face.—What have you been doing with yourselves all afternoon? Are you packed?

—Almost.

—I was thinking, said Hugo, digging into the cake,—I was thinking you should have a show. Up in town, I'm sure we could arrange it. That chap in Cork Street, he thought you were terrific.

Phyllida looked at him.

—What do you think? he asked her.—Do it now, I'd say, before things get tricky.

—What do you mean? asked Florence, wiping honey from her fingers.—What kind of tricky?

—He means the war, said Madeleine.—Don't you, Daddy?

—Of course, it might not happen. But I was thinking after lunch, how lucky we are here, so self-contained, all our fruit and veg—

—But won't you have to fight?

—Too old, said Hugo, and really felt it now, under Phyllida's gaze.

—I do not, she said slowly,—Want to have a show. Can you not understand that?

—Well, of course, if you're not ready . . .

—Not ready, not good enough. I don't even want to discuss it.

Hugo, averting his eyes from her gaze, caught the look between his daughters and felt his guts begin to knot.

—Well, now, he began, searching for a change of subject, and then, as a sudden pain, real pain, began to grip him, could not stop his groan, or the clutch at his bulging stomach.

—What? Daddy? What is it? Madeleine had her hand on his arm.

He closed his eyes, and felt himself swim into blackness.

—Put your head down, Phyllida commanded, and he did.

—Get him a glass of water, Flo, said Madeleine, and he heard her get up, and run over the grass.

—Daddy?

—I'm all right, he murmured, and waited for the water. When it came—Here you are, Daddy, here you are—he drank slowly, felt the life flood back.

—That's better. He wiped the back of his neck, opened his eyes, saw them all looking at him.—Sorry. I feel better now. He put the glass on the table, noticed his hand was trembling. Still—the pain was fading.

—Shouldn't have had that second pear, he said.—Indigestion, that's all.

—I'd leave that cake alone if I were you, said Phyllida.

44

—Quite right. Quite right. Well, now—where were we?

Nobody could remember, nor wanted to. And as he eased himself back into the afternoon, the bees sailing by and the sinking sun turning the windows of the house to gold, he thought how wonderful it was to feel well, it was all that mattered, that and having his family around him; and everything, in the end, would come right, he was sure of it.

Phyllida poured more tea, he kept to water. The cat came out from a long afternoon in the shade and everyone talked to her and about her. After a while, the girls got up and flopped down on the grass; after a while, they fell asleep.

—Sorry I was so tactless, he said to Phyllida.—About the show, I mean.

—It doesn't matter.

—Getting cooler, now.

She pulled her sunhat over her eyes and withdrew. And he sat there watching them all, his darlings, as the shadows deepened, and far above a little light aircraft came droning over from somewhere, leaving its smoky trail.

Outside the House

SUNDAY AFTERNOON. Autumn rain falls steadily on to the muddy water of the Thames, on the
rusting barges, the police launches, the bobbing black
buoys. I am walking along the South Bank, stopping by
the second-hand bookstalls under Waterloo Bridge, the
Riverfront restaurant of the BFI. Beneath the concert
halls, skateboarders are slamming and spinning in a concrete cave; ahead, the invisibly turning Eye, and Hunger-
ford Bridge, where the trains rumble and squeal, picking
up speed, heading for New Cross, Lewisham and Bexley
Heath.

Gulls swoop over the water, lights from the Riverfront
spill on to the cobbles. Inside, people are being directed to
their tables, or making for the bar. They have been to an
afternoon concert; they have been to watch old movies;
now they are talking over tea and pastries, and I stand by
a bookstall and watch them: the families, the groups of
friends, the couples; those who have come alone, and who
now turn again to their programmes, bury themselves in
the papers, look out at the falling rain. I have come alone,
but I'm not going in there now.

On Sunday afternoons, on weekdays after work, we
used quite often to be here, on the South Bank. Sometimes we went to hear chamber music in the Purcell
Room, more often to sit in the darkness of what was
then the National Film Theatre. We watched Bergman,

and Truffaut, and Pasolini; we watched films from Eastern Europe which outshone them all. I remember, from films made long before 1989, and liberation, trains, and snow, and shoe-shop girls; the menacing rustle of reeds by a silken river; the rustle of sheets in shuttered rooms. I remember the misty breath of cattle on winter mornings, a long dark line of men in suits, bearing a coffin through a mountain village: on the soundtrack were shuffling foot-steps, a single bell. I remember shipyards and sirens, a pregnant girl in a blue dress, a prison cell; running feet on wet streets, a gunshot. I remember how we used to turn and look at one another, and lean together, and look back at the screen.

My lover had an interest in Eastern Europe. He negoti-ated contracts for a pharmaceutical company moving into new markets: Warsaw, Budapest and Prague. Everything was opening up. We met at a conference I was covering for the scientific journal where I work: I liked him at once. He was a big, heavy man who talked well; he also had a gravity and stillness which I found compelling. I liked to arrive late for our appointments so that I could come upon him: reading, looking up at my approach, slowly closing his book and rising to greet me.

—All right?

—All right.

We kissed, we sat down, everything fell into place.

—What are you reading?

He read all the time, and especially when he was trav-elling; he also wrote poetry. He introduced me to some of the poets of Eastern Europe: Holub, Herbert, Czer-niawski. He was sensitive and thoughtful, a man of wide interests, several years older than me. I found his company and conversation enriching.

Around us people came and went. There was the rattle

of cutlery, the chink of glasses. We fell silent, and looked at one another. I craved his touch.

—Shall we go?

The rain has faded to drizzle; a fresh wind carries it away downriver. I remember a bedroom, curtained in daylight; a heavy, naked man, standing before me, holding out his arms.

I am consumed.

—I love you, I love you, I'll always love you—

And afterwards, as it grows dark, and he leans across to switch the light on, and reach for his book, and read to me—

—I don't know who I am any more, except with you.

—Sssh . . .

There are declarations one should never make. Such passion carries with it—from the very first moment of recognition, and delight, and fear—the implication of an ending, a casting out from heaven.

The riverside lamps have come on, pale globes in the fading light. It is too cold and damp to stay out much longer. I turn back, walking slowly. Leaves from the dripping plane trees cling to the ground, a riverboat goes by. When it has passed, I can hear water slap against the wall, and the steps of the pier, a sound as melancholy as the thin harmonica I hear up ahead, on the bridge.

Lapping water, a beggar's tune; the slam of carriage doors on an empty platform; reluctant footsteps, going home alone. Soundtrack of a Sunday in the city. I remember images from other films we saw together: a dark horse and carriage and enormous parasol on an endless stretch of sand; a squealing pig, and shouting voices; a worn wedding ring in a tiny box; an old man's smile, remembering happiness.

I stand looking down at the darkening water.

In the great, enduring marriages, there is passion and also partnership and peace. This is how I imagine it to be. There is a to and fro of kindness and consideration which goes deep. I compare such marriages to great houses: with time to spare, you can wander from room to quiet room, follow cool corridors to spacious kitchens, lofty dining rooms, with a place at the table for everyone. There is a study where you can be by yourself, there are doors which lead out to the graceful garden, and paths to the contemplation of water. They wind past a shrubbery, through a rose garden, back to the house, where fires are lit in the evenings. The house holds its history; there is a future ahead of it; much care goes into its preservation.

Great houses are rare, and few people live in them. Beyond their graceful gardens are wild, empty, uncultivated places, lonely and sometimes dangerous. The solid gate swings shut, keeping the fortunate safe. Those who are left outside it, with darkness falling, look about them fearfully.

Back at the flat, I put on the heating, cook something, try to eat it. I try to read.

Who was it who said that the whole of the world's literature is one great mating cry? Someone who knew what it was like to be unmated, out in the cold, calling, prowling, angry and afraid.

The poets of Eastern Europe, and many of those who have come to the city as exiles, have had more serious preoccupations, not least of them survival. Grief feels serious enough, and how shall I survive?

I wake, and the pillow is soaking. I sit up, howling in the dark.

I weep in the morning, in the queue at the bus stop on Rosebery Avenue. I weep when I am on the bus, and when I get off it, walking towards the continental newsagents on the corner of Grays Inn Road. It is raining again, and the rack of European newspapers flaps and bangs in the wind.

—You have a cold? asks the man from Eastern Europe in the kiosk. I have been buying my papers here for a long time.

—Yes, I say.—A terrible cold.

I pay for the paper, and blow my nose. I walk along to the offices of the scientific journal where I have been working for too long and am just holding down my job. No one else is here yet. I sit at my desk and sob.

It is *Grand Central Station*, it is *The Weather in the Streets*, it is my life, which has lost its meaning.

For weeks, a film of the past unreels before me and the tears pour out of me, as if my body and indivisible soul were made of water: welling, flowing, unstoppable.

There is sadness, and there is possession by grief.

On Wednesdays, after work, I see a therapist. I am sceptical and resistant, but I go each week: she has been recommended by a colleague whose opinions I respect. She is in her sixties: her family were German Jews who fled to London in 1938 —at our first meeting we make a connection, though after that she says little about her own life. She says little about anything in our early sessions: she listens, intently. Each week I get off the tube and walk to her house on a street in the heartland of psychoanalysis,

between Swiss Cottage and Belsize Park. I ring the door-
bell. I am taken to a consulting room on the upper floor.

I sit in a chair by a bookcase and close my eyes and the
film of the past plays out before me, fast and frightening.
I run it repeatedly, unstoppably.

A stolen afternoon, a bedroom with the curtains drawn.
A heavy naked man sits on the edge of the bed—my
bed—and draws me towards him.

—Do you want me to do this—

—Or this—

—Or this—

I have never been so intimate with anyone.

The light beyond the curtains fades. People are coming
home from work.

—Time for me to go, I'm afraid . . .

—He was married, says my therapist.

Of course he was married.

It grows colder. Christmas approaches.

At Christmas the windows of great houses blaze, and
church bells ring across the fields. There is dancing in the
hall, and fires crackle. Children run up and down in the
corridors, shrieking, rushing out into the garden leaving
the door to swing wide, letting the cold in, chided by
grown-ups, taking no notice.

Upstairs, in a neglected room, with fading curtains and
a patch of damp, a difficult child is hiding, and won't join
in. Her face is pressed to the glass, she is sullen and unap-
pealing. She is waiting for them all to call her, but no one
calls; her foot kicks against the wall beneath the mullioned
window, and old damp plaster crumbles and falls to the
floor. She grinds it into the rug, and kicks again.

I dream of this house, and of this child, repeatedly. I dream of my lover, walking away. I wake, and the pillow is soaking.

At work, I am asked to write a feature on recent research in cardiovascular disease. I go through conference papers, newspaper reports. The name of the company for which my lover works is printed in bold, bruise-black ink. I see it everywhere.

I see my lover, walking away from me.

—I have to do this—

—Don't go, don't go, don't go—

Colleagues remark on my appearance, and are kind. It is the season of parties. I creep home.

Christmas approaches. Cards fall on to the mat. I suppose I must send some. I send some. The city is packed, there are trees in every window. Everyone has somewhere to go. I know this is a fiction.

My mother telephones, wanting to know my plans. I tell her I am coming home, of course I am coming home, what else would I be doing—

I hang up, and guilt and a disproportionate rage make war within me. I pace, I pour a drink. I am becoming someone I do not wish to become.

—Who is this child in your dream? She must be there for a reason. There is always a reason for dreams. They show you a part of yourself, they can help to heal you—

I do not wish to see parts of myself in order to be healed. I was healed and made whole by my lover's touch. I would be healed now, by his touch—

There is sadness, and there is possession by grief. I am possessed, it is why I am here. I sit in the chair by the bookcase and talk, and listen. December wind rattles the window. Trees toss in the wind.

— Perhaps we should meet more often. She reaches for her diary. — Since there is to be this Christmas break —

I can hear her grandchildren, banging about in the basement. I can hear her husband, climbing the stairs, searching for something in another room. The disproportionate rage takes hold of me.

— I think you should have your consulting room elsewhere —

She looks at me. There is a silence.

— I am excluding you, I am shutting you away in an upper room, I am leaving you at Christmas to be with my own family, when you are already abandoned —

I am overcome by weeping.

— Who is the child in your dream?

I cannot speak.

She is the only child, put to bed too early —
who craves brothers and sisters —
who longs for her older lover —
the part of myself I cannot love —
the child I may never have —

That night, I dream of a house so dark I can barely see the outlines of the windows. It is matt black, sealed up, impenetrable. Someone has tied it up with white rope — up, down, across, knotted at every corner.

I have come to the end.

The path to recovery is long, and briars of thorn grow over it.

The city, so full, is suddenly empty. The last cards drop

on the mat. There is one from my lover, who says he is sorry. He is with his family.

It is where he should be, and I cannot bear it—
Enough.
Enough, enough, enough.

The last day at work. Drinks all round, kisses on the cheek and Happy Christmas.

I pack, I telephone my mother and tell her the time of the train. Carols are on the radio, my cousins and their children are coming for Christmas lunch.

I go out, and look for a taxi.

The platform is packed, everyone is in a hurry, the train is late. I find a seat, we pull out of the station. The lights flicker off, then on again. London is left behind.

My mother is there at the station to greet me. We embrace.

That night, I dream of a house growing dark as the sun goes down behind it. Wild geese beat through the sky. I can hear their cries, I can hear the beat of their wings, I watch them grow smaller, skimming the tops of bare trees: making for water, and another country.

Pegwell Bay

I T'S BINNIE, SHE said. — What's yours?—Binnie? That's not a name. He turned out another well-packed mound of sand, and knelt back on his heels. The castle still needed more turrets, but it was getting better. He began to scoop more of the damp sand into the bucket.

—Yes, it is, said Binnie.—Anyway, what's yours?

—Ian, if you want to know. That's a proper name. Binnie—it's just silly.

She looked down at her feet. Little rivers of sea were furrowing the sand into hard ridges, like a ploughed field. The tide was still far out, and the sky was grey and pale.

—Anyway, she said.—I bet I'm older than you.

—Bet you're not.

—Bet I am. How old are you, anyway?

—Anyway, anyway. Shan't tell you.

—Well, I'm eight, said Binnie.—I was eight last week.

Ian turned out another turret. He was getting hungry, and looked at his watch. His mother had given it to him last term, for his seventh birthday. He wasn't supposed to wear it on the beach.

—I'm going to finish this, he said,—and then I'm going to go home and have tea. And then I'll come back and finish this, and then it'll be late, and that proves I'm older than you, because I bet you don't stay up late. I should think you go to bed at six, or something.

— But look! Binnie almost shouted. — There's a crab!

Ian jumped up. — Where? Where is it?

It was very small. It lay on its back in one of the furrows of sand, its frail legs and pincers waving feebly. They bent down. Binnie looked at its stomach, criss-crossed with grooves, full of sand.

— I'm going to take it home.

— I'm having it, said Ian. — I collect crabs.

— But I want to collect this one! Very carefully, she turned it over. The crab lay still, then started to scuttle quickly down the furrow.

— Quick! shouted Ian. He grabbed his bucket and pounced down, scooping up the crab with a handful of sand. He dropped it in the bucket and Binnie peered in. It did not move.

— I think it's dead. You've killed it.

— No, I haven't, said Ian. — You're so silly — it's just recovering, that's all. I'm going to give it some water.

He began to walk towards a deeper pool in the sand. Binnie twisted her top round her middle, and then untwisted it again. She wanted to go to the lavatory.

— It's my crab! she called. — I found him.

Ian was bent over the pool, sloshing handfuls of water into the buck. She ran up.

— I said it's my crab. I want him.

— How do you know it's a him?

— He looks like a him. And I was going to give him a name, and keep him.

— You can't give a crab a name.

Binnie felt suddenly tired. Two large gulls landed just near them. They had bright cold eyes and long beaks, and they began to walk towards her.

— I'm going home now, she said. — You can keep him if you want.

She walked back to her sandals, lying like two brown animals in the sand. They were her old ones, especially for the beach. She was glad she didn't have to wear the new ones, anyway. They were stiff, with sharp buckles, and these were friends. She put them on, and began to walk along the cold sand, away from the gulls. Ian called after her.

—Hey! Why're you going?

—And where have you been? Her mother had her cross voice on. —It's past five, and your father's out looking for you. What did I tell you? Come on, what did I say?

—Be back for tea, said Binnie, looking at the sand.

—Don't mutter! That's the last time you go wandering off by yourself like that. Your poor father's on holiday—he's got better things to do than go looking everywhere for you.

—Yes, said Binnie.

—Well, don't just stand there. Come on and have your tea, and then it's bed.

—Do I have to go to bed? Can't I stay up?

—Stay up? Certainly not. Dad and are going out tonight, I've told you. We're not spending the evening stuck in the chalet. We're going to the pub, and you can just go to sleep.

—But what if I feel sick? asked Binnie, twisting her top.

—Why ever should you feel sick? Don't start playing up. There's Mrs Lewis next door, she'll keep an eye on you. But I don't want to hear you've been any trouble, mind. Now come and sit down.

Binnie perched on a thin-legged stool at the table. It was small, and covered with a blue-checked plastic cloth, and from the stool she could see out of the chalet window.

The sea was coming in, and the sky was darker. A man was walking past with a big hairy dog. — Come along, boy, she heard him say. — Looks like rain.

Her mother set a plate of baked beans and an egg on toast in front of her, and poured a glass of squash. The egg looked like an old egg. It had started to curl up at the edges, and its yellow eye was covered with a sort of skin. The beans looked furry, like beans did when you left them in the saucepan a long time.

— I'm not very hungry, she said. Her mother didn't answer. She was in the dark little bedroom at the back. Binnie poked at the beans with her fork, and tried some. They tasted thick and warm and not very nice. Very quietly, she slid off the stool and picked up the plate. She carried it outside the door, and round the side where the grass was stiff and tough, and prickled her legs. There was a little gap underneath the chalet, a secret gap for hiding things. She scraped the beans and the one-eyed egg off the plate and under the gap.

— And what are you doing, my lass?

Binnie jumped. Her father stood there, just watching, as she stood up and clutched the empty plate, streaked with bits of fat and sauce from the beans. How long had been there? She didn't dare look at his face. She just looked up as far as the top of his trousers, where the braces were fastened, and then down again.

— Um — nothing.

Her father bent down and took the plate. — Didn't like it?

— Wasn't hungry.

— Binnie! her mother shouted from inside. She came out and looked around.

— She's out here with me, love. Her father motioned Binnie inside, holding the plate behind him. As they went in, he popped it back on the table and it just sat there, as if it had never been away. Her mother never even saw. She was wearing different clothes: a frock with lots of flowers on, and a pair of high heels. She smelt different, too.

—Well, said her father.—You look nice, love. Her mother smiled at him—it wasn't an ordinary smile.

—Right, then, she said to Binnie.—Bed for you. Finished your supper?

—Can I have an apple?

—I thought you weren't hungry. All right, you can have an apple in bed. Now get undressed, quickly.

—But can I have a story?

—No, I've told you—we're going out. You can read by yourself at your age, can't you?

Binnie went into her bedroom. It was even smaller than the one her parents had, just room for a narrow bed, a thin-legged chair, and a wobbly little table. Bear was sitting on the bed in his pyjamas. He looked a bit lonely. Binnie picked him up and stroked his ears.

—I've been by myself all day, said Bear.—And you didn't even take off my pyjamas.

—I know. I'm sorry. She pulled off her top.—When we're in bed I'll tell you a story. I've got to get undressed now.

She pulled off her shorts and knickers and unfastened the sandals, brushing the sand off her toes. She put on her own pyjamas, which were a bit tight under the arms, and went into the bathroom. There was no window at all in here. It was a poky place, between her room and her parents'. There was a long piece of string that you pulled to switch the light on. Binnie sat on the lav. Then she got off and washed her face and cleaned her teeth.

She looked at herself in the mirror as she rubbed the brush up and down. Her hair was like a little cap;

it needed brushing, and it looked even lighter—perhaps
it was the sun, yesterday, that had done that. She took a
mouthful of water and sloshed it round her mouth and
spat it out. Then she took another mouthful, and began,
very quietly, to gargle *God Save the Queen*. She had learnt
how to gargle and hum at the back of her throat at the
same time, last term, when they were all practising for
the Coronation. Her father had hung a flag out of the
window, like everyone else. But no one else at school
could do gargle-and-hum.

— Binnie! called her mother. — Whatever are you
doing?

She spat out the water. She could hear Bear wondering why she was being so long. Surely he must remember
about the trick. She went over to the lav and took hold
of the chain, then she walked backwards towards the door
and stretched her other arm out and took hold of the
string from the light. If she pulled the chain now, and then
ran out and didn't pull the light off until she was outside
the door, she'd be safe. If she didn't, the wolves that hid
right down at the bottom of the lav would get her. When-
ever she pulled the chain, they roared. She pulled it now,
as hard as she could, then ran, pulling the light string with
her. She ran straight up against her mother, hard.

— Whatever are you doing? she asked again.

— Sorry, said Binnie. — It's the wolves.

— Wolves? I'll give you wolves if you aren't in bed in
one minute, I can tell you that.

Binnie ran into her room, jumped into bed and grabbed
Bear, pulling him under the bedclothes. Her father came
in with the apple on a patterned plate: he'd cut it into
pieces.

— Here you are, love, he said. — Be all right, will you?

— Of course she'll be all right, said her mother. She

had put on some lipstick and some more of that perfume. It smelt very strong. Binnie wrinkled her nose. —Funny smell, said Bear, from under the bedclothes. She pinched him to be quiet.

—Goodnight, she said. —Have a nice time. I don't feel sick.

—Of course you don't. Now, you can read for just a bit, then Mrs Lewis will come in and turn your light out. And you're to be good, and go to sleep at once.

Her mother went out of the room.

Her father bent down and gave her a kiss. He'd slicked up his hair and was wearing his jacket.

—See you in the morning.

—See you in the morning, said Binnie. —I found a crab today.

—Did you, love? He shut the bedroom door.

After Mrs Lewis had come and switched off the light, said goodnight and told her to be good, Binnie lay for a long time comforting Bear, who had earache. At last he fell asleep, crooked into her arm.

Binnie lay awake. She could hear the sea, much closer now. It was making a roaring sound. Like the wolves. Were they still crouched down inside the lav? It had started to rain, and the whole chalet was making strange creaking noises.

No one was out on the front now. She couldn't even hear the wireless from next door. It must be very late.

Roar, rrrroarrrr, went the sea. Binnie lay absolutely still.

—Hello.

— 'lo. Ian went on digging.

It was very sunny, and the sea didn't look frightening at all this afternoon. There were lots of little waves jumping about, and people were out in boats, with coloured sails.

And there were more people on the beach than yesterday, rubbing on Nivea cream, getting undressed behind stripy windbreaks. She could see the man with the big hairy dog walking along by the water. He'd hung his shoes round his neck by the laces, and the dog was running in and out of the sea, barking and splashing.

—How's the crab?

—It's all right. It's in a bowl in my bedroom.

—Is it? Won't your mother be cross?

—No, why should she be? He was building another castle, but much bigger than yesterday's. It had a wall all round it, with a gap to get through, and then a moat.

—Actually, he said,—she's called it Percy.

—Called it what?

—Percy. It's a silly name. He stood up.—This castle is going to be the biggest and the best and the most enormous castle you've ever seen.

Binnie flopped down on the sand.—It does look very big, already. Are you going to have a battle in it?

—Might.

—Can I put shells on it? They lay all around her, her fingers itched.

—No.

Footsteps came towards them, over the sand and the shells: Binnie looked up. A tall woman wearing a funny green dress was walking along the beach. She had thick dark hair down to her shoulders, no grips or anything, and she was carrying a bag made out of different bits of material, all sewn together.

—Hello, she said to Ian.—I thought I'd come and see how you're getting on. She smiled at Binnie.—Are you Ian's friend?

—Don't know.

—She's called Binnie, said Ian, filling his bucket again.

— Hello — Binnie? said the mother. — That's a nice name.

— No, it isn't, said Ian. He was patting the walls of the castle. — It's stupid, it's even worse than Percy.

— Well, I like it. His mother sat down beside them and pulled a book out of the bag. — Is it short for something?

— It's short for Belinda, but I don't like it, and anyway, when I was little I couldn't say it properly, and it sort of came out Binnie.

— Anyway, anyway, anyway! sang Ian. He danced round the walls of the castle, waving his bucket. — I'm going down to the rocks to collect things.

— What sort of things? asked Binnie.

— Oh, just things. I might find another crab, for all you know.

— I'll come too.

— No, you can't. I don't want you to. You'll be a nuisance.

He picked up the bucket and spade and she watched him walk down towards the rocks. He had a funny kind of face: very dark, and pointed. He made her think of some kind of animal she'd seen in a book.

— Never mind, said his mother. — You can stay and talk to me. My name's Elizabeth.

— Like the Queen. I've got a Coronation mug at home.

— Have you? And where are you staying?

Binnie pointed back towards the row of chalets. Everyone had their doors open wide today.

— Up there, in one of those shallys, with my mother and father.

— Where are they now?

— My mother's gone into town to the shops. And my father's somewhere over there. He fell asleep.

She could just make him out, in his deckchair. She picked up a stick someone had dropped—perhaps the hairy dog. She drew patterns in the sand, long swirly lines. Then she tried to draw a crab, but it wouldn't come out right.

—Here, said Elizabeth, and leant over and drew a little round crab with sticking-out legs, and eyes on long stalks, and wrote—'Percy' underneath.—Can I draw you? she asked.

—What, in the sand?

—No, on a piece of paper. She opened her book, and Binnie saw it was a sketchbook, with a pencil tucked into a rubber band. Elizabeth turned the pages, found an empty one.

—Now, you just carry on making patterns, and I'll draw you.

—And then I'll draw you, said Binnie.

Elizabeth laughed. It was a lovely laugh.

—Hey! shouted Ian.—Hey, hey, hey!

They looked up. Out on the rocks, he was waving to them.

—Come and see!

—Come on, then, said Elizabeth, and they got up and began walking towards him.

—I've found a pool with something extraordinary in it, he said, as they drew close.

—How exciting, said Elizabeth.—Let's have a look. Mind yourself on the rocks, Binnie. She took her hand. They clambered across to where Ian was now hunched over a deep pool, and bent down.

The water was very clear, but dark at the bottom. And from the side of a rock something bright and wavy was floating, floating but clinging to the rock. Red—no, a strange, dark fleshy pink, with long wavy whips feeling the water.

—Isn't that perfect? said Elizabeth.

—I know what it is, said Binnie. —It's a Nemony. I saw one in a book.

—Is it a Nemony? Ian asked Elizabeth.

—Yes, Binnie's quite right, that's exactly what it is. A sea-anemone. You are clever, Ian, to find it.

—I'm going to take it home, he announced. —To put with the crab.

—But you can't, darling. It isn't like a crab. Do you see? It lives clinging on to the rock like that, and if you take it away, you'll hurt it. It might even die.

—No! cried Binnie. —I don't want it to die.

—Well, it won't, said Elizabeth, brushing her hair back. —Not if we just leave it there. And perhaps when we come back tomorrow it'll still be here, waiting for us. Oh, isn't it lovely? I'd like a frock like that. All deep pink and floaty.

—But I want to take it home, said Ian.

—I know what we'll do now, said Elizabeth. —We'll go back to the castle before the sea comes in, and finish it off, and then Binnie can come back and have tea —if her parents will let her.

—No, said Ian. —I want to stay here and—and look at it.

—So do I, said Binnie. But she wanted to go back with Elizabeth, too.

—Well, you can both stay here for a bit longer, then. Elizabeth got to her feet. —And I'll go back to the castle, and guard it. But don't be too long.

Binnie watched her clamber carefully over the rocks, and then walk up the beach to the castle. The sun was really very hot now, and bright, and she had to screw her eyes up. Right along the beach she could just see her father, reading the paper. Did he know where she was? She turned back to Ian. He was poking the Nemony with a piece of dried-up seaweed. It was all closed up now, and solid, like a boiled sweet.

— Oh, do leave it! she said.

Elizabeth lay in the sun with her eyes shut. She was half-asleep, hearing but hardly conscious of the gulls, children shouting, a noisy game of cricket. The pages of her sketch-book lifted, as someone ran past, and she put out a hand to keep them still. Was it any good, her drawing? Such an intent little thing gazing down at her work — none of Ian's urgency or fierceness.

Gulls cried above her, people were making tea on the beach. From somewhere came the smell of a primus, the clatter of a tin teapot, then the sudden sweet scent of an orange. What did that make her think of?

A picnic, a stolen afternoon. Trees in a field, with cows standing motionless in the shade. And the two of them, kissing and kissing, entwined on the rug on the grass, she and Ian's father, whom she had allowed herself to love, and who, at the end of the war, had gone back to his wife.

— I have to do. He sat there, the end of the picnic all around them, his head in his hands. Flies buzzed around in the sun.

What would he feel, after all this time, if he knew he had a son? She shook her head. Why should she want to cry for him, today? For over seven years she had managed, bringing up a little boy who hardly took after her at all. She'd never imagined it would be a boy.

There were all sorts of things out on the rocks: Binnie couldn't think why she'd never been out there before. She would tell Bear about the Nemony tonight—he'd seen the picture, too. And there were barnacles, and limpets, which clung fast to the rock the moment you touched them. Ian had tried to prise one off, but even with his spade he couldn't. There was a special seaweed with bubbles in it, that went pop, when you pressed them. A little bit of water came out with each pop.

—Look, said Ian.—These are mussels. You can eat them, if you want.

—No, you can't, she said.—You can't eat anything out of the sea like that. You have to cook things before you can eat them.

—That's not true. There's a boy in our class who says you can eat mussels raw. He told me. You just open it up, and scrape it out, and eat it.

—I'll ask my father. She stopped and thought for a moment.—Where's your father?

—Haven't got one.

There was a girl at school who hadn't got a father. He'd run away and left them. She said it was ever so much better since he'd gone.

—Did he run away? she asked.

—Mind your own business.

—But did he?

—Shut up. Here, have a mussel. Go on.

—No. I don't want one.

—Then you can't come and play with me, ever again. So there.

Binnie looked at the mussel. Ian had got it open, or perhaps it had been open on the rocks already, soaking up the sun. Some of them were. It looked quite pretty inside, soft and thick, like coffee ice cream. There was a little orange bit on it.

—Oh, go on, he said.—It won't hurt you.

—You have some first.

—No, you go first. Go on, and then you can go on playing with me. But if you don't, I'll never speak to you again.

Binnie stretched out her hand.—All right. She poked her finger into the shell. The mussel felt slimy.

—Ugh.

—Oh, eat it.

She dug it out and put it in her mouth. It was salty, and when she bit on it it was chewy, and difficult to swallow. Then it just slithered down.

—I did it, she said.—It's gone.

—Good, said Ian.—Have another.

Elizabeth was far out at sea, standing alone at the stern of a strange, square ship, with black railings. Far out in the distance she could see an island, half-shrouded in mist. Just rocks, nothing else, but they weren't ordinary rocks; they were very pale, and beautiful, and she wanted to reach them more than anything in the world.

And then she saw the porpoises. She almost stopped breathing. They were a deep, mysterious, wonderful blue, and they leapt higher and higher into the air, making great arcs, silently, in front of the ship. As she watched them, a low humming seemed to envelop everything—the sea, the ship, the rocky island: distant, and eerie. Higher and still higher the porpoises leapt, arching up into the sea air, spraying her face with icy water. The island was moving away now, further and further.

She opened her eyes. Ian was standing beside her, sprinkling water on to her face from his bucket.

—Oh, he said.—You are awake.

—I am now, said Elizabeth.—Have you had a nice time? Where's Binnie?

—Gone home. I'm starving.

—So am I, now I think about it. She pulled herself up.—The tide's come in a lot. Thank goodness you got back. Fool, fool, she told herself, as she gathered up their things. Anything could have happened.

The sun was getting very low now, melting into the sea. They walked away up the beach.

As the tide came in, the castle walls slowly crumbled and fell. A wave rushed into the moat, licking its sides. By the time Elizabeth and Ian had reached the front, most had slumped away.

—I feel sick, said Bear.

—So do I, said Binnie.—Very.

She pulled him closer, and tried not to think about it. It wasn't as dark as last night: the sky was clear and there was a moon, though she couldn't see it from her bed, just the pale chilly light of it in a patch on the floor. And the sea was quiet—all she could hear was a soft whooshing sound. It was quite peaceful, really, not like last night. If only she didn't feel so sick. She closed her eyes tight.

—Bear, she said,—I feel awful.

The wireless next door was annoying. At least she knew Mrs Lewis was up, listening. But she couldn't hear it properly, only a dreadful blur of words she couldn't make out. Her head was starting to spin. When would her parents be back?

Perhaps the sea wasn't so peaceful, after all. It was going up and down, up and down all the time. Why couldn't it ever be still? There was a great big mussel in her head, blue-black and very fierce, and it wouldn't go away. Then it was in her tummy, and her tummy was going up and down like the sea. She opened her eyes and sat up.

—I'm going to be sick, Bear, she said.—I have to go

to the bathroom. Bear just lay there. — You're coming too, said Binnie. — Please come with me.

She took his paw and started to get out of bed. But her head was full of mussel again, and then there were lots and lots of them, and there was an awful pain in her tummy, and suddenly she couldn't get any further.

— Help, she said faintly. The wireless next door mumbled and buzzed. — Help, said Binnie. There was something horrible at the back of her throat. She tried to get to the floor, the patch of moon started spinning, and then the room went dark.

She could hear voices. — My God, I've never seen such a mess. Couldn't you have got to the bathroom?

— Don't be cross with her, love. She does look poorly.

— I should think I'll be poorly, too, by the time I've cleared this up. Christ, who'd have a kid? Just look at the bedclothes.

Binnie opened her eyes. — I couldn't help it, she said.

— Well, get up now. Come on. Go on, Frank, you take her to the bathroom and give her a wash.

— Come on, Binnie, love. He took her hand.

But she felt so strange, standing up. The light was on, but she couldn't see anything because it was all spinning round so much.

— I — I . . .

Her father picked her up, and her head fell on his shoulder. They went into the bathroom and he stood her in front of the basin. Binnie started to cry. Then she was sick on the bathmat.

Ian was making a sandman. It had been Elizabeth's idea, when he got tired of building castles.

SUE GEE

—You can use shells for his eyes, and I'll look for a razor shell. That can be his mouth.
—Why did the razorbill raise her bill?
—I don't know. Why?
—So that the sea urchin could see her chin.
Elizabeth laughed.—Where did you find that?
—In the *Beano*.
—Well, you start a sandman, and I'll go and look for a razor shell.

She set off along the beach. It was chilly again today. Except for that one sunny day when they'd met Binnie, the weather had been relentlessly grey and cold. She pulled her jacket closer. There were few people about, and they were huddled in little knots. The gulls were wheeling overhead, a light wind tugging their cries out to sea. Why did everything look as if she'd seen it before?
—I know, she said.—*Pegwell Bay.*

She hadn't thought of that painting for years. Not since she was at art school, all those years ago. But when she was twenty, and saw it in the Tate Gallery for the first time, she'd just stopped still and gazed. What was it that made it stand out so, from all the other Victorian paintings? Just a flat grey beach at low tide, a receding line of cliffs, dark rocks. Women bent to gather shells, and a child stood alone, a little girl, gazing out of the picture, wearing—what? A dark hat, open coat, boots.

Faintly, in the distance of the sky, hung a comet, something marvellous and strange, the occasion of the picture, she remembered now. It was as if everything gathered there were waiting for it: the women in their cloaks, the light upon the sea, that child, looking out and away. But oh, there was something so lonely and sad about her, that quiet, mournful face in that cold grey weather. PEGWELL BAY, KENT A RECOLLECTION OF OCTOBER 5TH, 1858.

Specific though it was in time and place, the feeling the painting had given her was of something out of time, haunting and lost.

A child was walking alone down the beach. Elizabeth ran up to her.

—Binnie! Where've you been hiding? We haven't seen you for days.

—I've been ill, said Binnie.

—Have you? My God, you do look pale. What was wrong?

—I had Food Poisoning. I was very sick. The doctor had to come in the middle of the night.

—Oh, you poor little thing. However did you get that?

—It was the mussels— But Binnie stopped. Somehow she didn't want to tell Elizabeth that Ian had given them to her. Made her eat them. —It doesn't matter, she said. —I'm better now. But we're going home tomorrow. My mother says it's the worse holiday she's ever had.

Elizabeth looked at her. She looked so thin, and she'd been thin to start with. Before she knew what she was doing, she'd picked her up and hugged her. Why did she feel like crying again?

She swallowed. —I'll tell you what. Now you're better, and as it's your last day, why don't you come and have lunch with us? I've got some tomato soup in a Thermos and some sandwiches. Can you see over there? Ian's building a sandman. Come on.

—I can't, said Binnie. —I've promised. Not to go wandering off again.

There was quite a breeze now, and Elizabeth's hair was blowing in front of her eyes. Binnie pushed it away.

—But where are your parents?

—Packing up. They just sent me out for some fresh air. But I've got to go back—really.

—All right. Elizabeth put her down. —Well, she said. —I don't suppose we shall see each other again. She held out her hand. —Goodbye, Binnie.

—Goodbye—Elizabeth. Thank you.

—For what?

—For asking me. She let go of Elizabeth's hand, and walked back up the beach towards the row of chalets. —Goodbye, she said again, not looking round.

Elizabeth watched her go. Then she turned back towards Ian. The sandman had grown a lot, she could see from here. She still hadn't found a razor-shell.

In the late afternoon, Binnie walked down towards the sea. She did feel better outside. The chalet was so hot with the oil stove on, it made her head feel thick. And she knew she was in the way while the packing went on, especially since her father had gone to get the tickets.

—You're really getting on my nerves, her mother said.

The tide was coming in, but there was still quite a lot of beach left. Binnie wasn't looking at the sea, though. She was looking for shells. She was going to take them home, and stick them on a box: she'd seen a shell box in a shop on the front, and it looked very pretty. She would keep things in it. Or give it to her mother.

—I made this for you, she would say.

She knelt down, and started to gather the largest shells she could find. There were a lot, really. It was quite difficult to choose, and she couldn't carry that many in the pockets of her shorts or they'd get crushed. The sand had made those little furrows again. Oh, and there was a crab!

Very gently she picked him up. He was even smaller than Percy, and he lay in her hand hardly moving at all.

He had a reddish-brown back and very, very small pincers. This time she was going to keep him—otherwise a gull would get him, she knew. She could hear them now, very noisy and harsh in the sky.

Binnie looked up. Far away along the beach she could see Ian and Elizabeth, walking towards the sea. It looked very pale, like the sky, and in a place farther out there hardly seemed to be any difference between them at all. Somewhere inside her Binnie had a strange sort of feeling—an emptiness.

A ship was moving along the bit where the sea and the sky just met. Smoke blew from the chimney, as if someone had drawn it. Then it sailed slowly away.

Annunciation

T HE KITCHEN WAS filled with a clear plain light.
When she rinsed the white plates and set them up
on the rack, when she wiped the draining board, she saw
how all the subdued colours of the room—the pale wood
of the rack and board and table, the red tiled floor, the
faded blue of the tea towel hung over the range—were
unified by this light, all of a good plain piece, and this
pleased her, because so much of the house was dark.

It stood by the church, and the shadow of the tower
fell over the garden. Yew, and a great dense fir spread
over the churchyard, and the yew was as tall as the tower.

That was the side on which her bedroom lay. All
through her life, the clock had chimed, and the wind had
moved through the boughs of the fir, and when she was a
child she had often been afraid of a winter's storm at night,
and everything blew and creaked and rang, and she had
cried out for her mother.

—Here I am. Her mother came along the landing in
her red woollen dressing gown, with her hair let down
and a candle.—Here I am. She smoothed Morag's hair
and sat down in the chair, and together they listened to
the wind and rain as the candle dripped and burned.

—Fire and sleet and candlelight, and Christ receive my
soul, said her mother.—My grandfather used to say that,
when we had a storm at home. She kissed her, and said it
would soon be morning. Then she went out, and back to

her own room, where Father was. It was thirty-four steps away, with not a gleam of light between here and there.

—Fire and sleet and candlelight, said Morag, as the wind blew over the churchyard and her window shook. She held fast to the quilt, and her heart hammered.

The house stood in such a strange position. She knew of no other like it. That was why her parents had come here: that's what her mother used to say: We have come to a house unlike any other. On the one side there was the church, and the towering trees; on the other, beneath the highest wall, was a great broad grassy path, running all the way past the garden to the village street at one end and a farmer's field at the other. The field led down to the river, and in summer the cattle sometimes stood in it, cooling down beneath the trees at the end of the day. When Morag was a child, she used to hang on the gate and watch them, after school. Everything down here opened out beneath the sky.

The stone wall which ran by the path was twelve feet high. On the other side lived a childless couple who kept themselves to themselves. So all through her childhood, it had been just she and her parents. Standing in the kitchen now, her whole being concentrated into these momentous hours, she let herself into the past.

—Morag! Morag! Their voices were like church bells, calling from this place and that within the house.—Morag!
—Here I am!

There were things to be done which she must do. Even when she was little she had her duties: to help take down the washing from the line, to put it away when her mother had ironed it all. To clean out the rabbit hutch. Oh, what a splendid great fellow he was, that rabbit. He would have been a comfort in a storm at night, but of course he couldn't come into the house.

—Please! He might be afraid, out there in the dark.

—He's a good strong rabbit. He'll be just fine.

What else did she have to do? Tidy her bedroom, take her father's cup of tea to him, when she came home from school. She carried the cup and saucer carefully across the hall, never spilling a drop. She set it down on the hat stand, knocked on the door of the study.

—Come in.

Her father sounded as if he were miles and miles away. She turned the handle, carried the cup, watched him complete a sentence. Then he looked up. The draught from the hall stirred the flames in the fire, lifted the page on his desk. Carefully, carefully, she set down the cup. He took off his glasses; she let him kiss her. — Thank you, Morag. The books on his desk were like tombstones, so heavy and old. His beautiful handwriting went on for page after page. The room smelled of wood smoke and ink.

—Go and have your tea now.

—Yes, Father.

She sat at the plain wooden table and ate her sandwich, and her mother sat beside her.

—What did you do today?

The noise of the schoolyard faded: the beat of the skipping rope, the shouts of the boys, the jangle of the big brass bell. Now she was home again, an only child. I am an only child, she said to herself, tucking her ankles together, drinking her milk. I live in a house unlike any other.

—We made a frieze, she said. — A frieze of Switzerland. We all had to draw Swiss things, and cut them out. I drew an alpine flower called a gentian. Ninian MacRae drew a cow with a bell. Miss MacHardy stuck everything up on the mountainside with glue.

Her mother smiled. She rolled out pastry for a pie, fluting the edges. Morag watched her. Her hands were always busy, sewing on buttons, basting a seam, addressing envelopes. Everything came from her, everything was plain and calm.

— When I grow up, I shall be like you, said Morag.

The pie went into the oven, and she sat on her mother's lap and leaned against her. She wound a skein of hair round the top button of her mother's cardigan, so she would have to be untied.

— You might be like your father. You might be a scholar.

Morag did not say, I am a little afraid of my father. She did not dare. He mother held her close. The years of her childhood went by.

When she was ten, her mother fell ill. When she was twelve, she died. When this happened, Morag felt all the darkness of the world heave up from the yawning depths of the earth and take her into it. Then, because she had been brought up with certainty and solidity and endless love, she grew up very fast, and learned to keep house for her father. She learned how to be with him, in his great loneliness and grief. They did the garden together, they ate together in the kitchen, and on Sundays in the dining room, where all the portraits were: grandparents, great-grandparents, great aunts and uncles, all in oil and sepia, all such a long way away in the past, or a long way down over the border. Her father was the last Scot to stay up here: everyone else had gone south. He used to say that everything he needed was in this house: his books, his wife, his daughter. When Morag grew up, she knew she could never leave him.

But now—
   Ah, now—

Her mother had died in 1921. The twenty-third of March, 1921. Ever since, when they got the new calendar at Christmas, and hung it on the hook beside the range, Morag had felt the date burned into it, scored into it, printed in darker type than all the other days, waiting for her and her father to get through it. Then they got through it, and she made herself think of other things.

Now it was September 1933, and now she had another thing to think about.

She put up the last white plate in the rack, and watched it catch the light. Then she let all the water gurgle away, and dried her hands. The grandfather clock in the hall struck two; just a second later the clock in the tower rang out. We are ahead of the church in this house, thought Morag, and hoped it was true. And now she had only two hours to wait.

She leaned against the railing on the range and felt its warmth against her back, and pressed her lips together on a smile, feeling happiness and excitement rise within her, stronger than the fear.

It was three o'clock. Her father was in the study. Out here in the garden, through the open window, she could hear him: turning papers, opening drawers in his desk. She was weeding, and raking the first fall of leaves. She put everything into the barrow and wheeled it down to the corner where they'd always had their bonfires. She tipped it all up, felt the weight of it all, and wondered for a moment if she should be doing these things, just now, if perhaps she should be careful. Then she thought: I am strong, and my mother is watching over me, just as she had said to herself all her life.

And she stood at the bottom of the garden, and felt the first wind of autumn blow over everything: the house, her mother's grave in the churchyard, the garden and the field beyond, where the cattle were; as she had done all her life. She lit the bonfire.

At the back of the house, here on the garden side, was its other distinctive feature: an arbour, pressed up against the wall, leafy and secret, in which you could sit, and watch the garden grow, and hear the approach down the grassy path of anyone who came calling.

Who came calling?

Her heart began to hammer.

When did a friend become a lover? How had someone she had known all her life—watched kicking a ball about with the other boys in the schoolyard, drawing a cow with a bell, greeted after church, waved to as he spun past on his old black bicycle—how did that person all at once seem different? And she had seemed different to him, he'd told her, lifting her hand to his lips. They'd both been down in the village one day, a day like any other, he with his bicycle propped up against the wall, the post office cat asleep on the counter, a couple of magpies making a racket, up on the roof.

—Two for joy, he said, as they waited in the queue, he with a great big parcel he was posting for his mother to her sister in Edinburgh, that was what he said, and she for her father's stamps and sealing wax. And they were just passing the time of day, as you did, there in the queue with everyone she knew, the magpies going *chatchatchat-chatchat* outside—and then, when she came out, he was just there in the sun with his bicycle, waiting.

Four o'clock. Deep inside the house came the chime of the grandfather clock. Then came the clock in the tower. Tonight they would be ringing the bells, in the weekly practice. She waited. Smoke from the bonfire was rising to the sky. She heard in the quiet the squeak of his brakes as he pulled up, then the steady *tick tick* as he wheeled the bicycle up the grassy path. He propped it up against the great high wall; he pushed open the gate; he walked up here to the arbour.

He looked like an angel in that old white shirt with the light behind him, so tall as he stood before her. And she thought again: this is love, this is love, as they said to one another over and over again, lying down there in the field by the river, gazing at one another, seen only by the cattle filing slowly past; kissing and doing—

Everything.

He looked down at her; she looked up at him. The air was full of smoke and silence.

—I have something to tell you, she said.

Heading North

I T C A M E T O Anthea like an epiphany—an illuminated moment, a life transformed: standing there on
the concourse of King's Cross station, at half-past two
on a Friday afternoon, about to board the train for Edinburgh. Around her strangers came and went; above her,
disembodied voices made announcements. Anthea, a
married woman of medium height and ordinary appearance, a university librarian in her forties, who for a long
time had thought there was nothing she could do about
her life, was visited by a realisation.

When Jason, her son, had left school, her husband,
James, would leave her.

There. It was a certainty. He was waiting only for that.

Beyond the concourse, out beyond dusty plane trees,
traffic roared along the Euston Road. Here, a disembodied voice made apologies for a delay. Nothing to do with
Edinburgh, nothing to do with her. It was not, at this
moment, clear what did have to do with her any more.
She could see Jason, just over there in Smiths, leafing
through a computer magazine. Yesterday, he had broken
up for the Easter holidays. Today, they were going to visit
Dorothy, Anthea's aunt, the first visit since he was four.
Then, he had worn dungarees and a Gap Kids T-shirt,
and been difficult on the train. Now he wore an iPod and
chewed gum relentlessly. He was fourteen years old and,
like her husband, spoke the bare minimum.

Sometimes, in the university library, Anthea leaned against the glass of the narrow windows between the book stacks, and felt glass surround her. She felt as if she were invisibly imprisoned, unable to move, or break out — unable, it sometimes seemed, to breathe. These moments were high and light and airless. Sometimes they felt like glimpses of spiritual enlightenment, and sometimes like the symptoms of a panic attack. They quickly passed, and Anthea, afterwards, paid them little attention, going about her work as usual.

The library itself she occasionally thought of a prison, so long had she been there, so routine were her days. She smiled at postgraduate students on the enquiry desk, issued books and ID cards, called up titles and searched for abstracts. After so many years, she was one of the senior members of staff, responsible not just for these everyday tasks, but for ordering stock in Renaissance Studies, and for training, but from time to time she still, at the end of the day, wheeled trolleys along the industrial grey carpet, and stacked the shelves.

The narrow windows let in shafts of light, the telephone rang at the desk, the doors at the far end swung open and shut, pages turned and voices faded. All these sounds, and all these ends-of-days — sliding the books into their places, running an eye over worn spines in indigo and parchment, plum and coniferous green — they wove in and out of one another, creating a pattern and texture, and there were occasions when Anthea, pausing, listening, felt the routine as a sweet, sustaining rhythm, and the library not a prison but a place of sanctuary. But these occasions, like those when she pressed her face against glass, feeling everything around and within her come to a halt — they passed, she forgot them. She got on with things — at work, and at home, where James and Jason came and went, pausing to eat, or watch the news, or text, or make a phone call.

Anthea had a colleague in the library called Edna, who lived alone. She viewed Anthea's married, maternal state with wistfulness.

—Nice weekend? she would ask of a Monday, fingering her necklace as they stood by the coffee machine.—How are the family?

—Fine, thanks, said Anthea, taking her cup. She said the same to Dorothy, in birthday and Christmas cards—James and Jason are well, and send their love. She said the same to her friends, women closer than Edna in age and experience, with whom she lunched, or went to a film. Sometimes these friends, speaking of their own lives, made intimate disclosures, but Anthea never did that. She had been brought up not to question, or answer back, or talk about the family to people outside. It was a background which equipped her well to live with James, who was often, she felt, unreasonable, as her father had often been.

For a while, when younger, encouraged by her more outspoken friends, she had tried to fight this inclination to please, to appease. Soon after Jason was born, she gave up, and gave in. Resisting meant tears, raised voices, exhaustion. She was already exhausted. She did what James and Jason asked, and read a lot. When friends confided, and waited for her to do the same, she smiled, like Tom the cabin boy, and said nothing. There was, in truth, little to disclose. Distance, silence, absence: what could you say about those?

But didn't she mind the absence? asked her friends. If James was always working, didn't she—didn't she—

She was used to it, Anthea told them, and it was true.

James took a lover. She took an aspirin, and told no

one. He came in late, but he had always come in late. She turned her face to the wall, and feigned sleep, as she feigned contentment to her friends. She did not speak about her discovery — the letters, the declarations — just as James had not spoken of their existence.

My life has closed down, she thought sometimes, lying awake beside her sleeping husband. My life has come to a halt, and there is nothing I choose to do about it. I carry on. With children, that is what you do. It was what her mother had done, and Anthea did not know how to break out of her long-dead mother's embrace. In the twenty-first century there are still women like this, and she was one of them.

So. There she was, until this shining moment. Half-past two on King's Cross station, and the train due to leave in fifteen minutes. Time they were off. And here was her realisation — was epiphany the word? Was she gazing up at the dazzling heavens, or into a yawning pit? When Jason left — when James left — what would become of her? She pictured the empty house, the cats. Well: it was often empty now, and she cherished the cats. But the days had a shape — the slam of the door after breakfast, as James left for the office, and Jason for school; the key in the lock as they came home again, one by one. They did, still, come home. When she turned her own key, after a late shift, there was sometimes one of them there. At weekends they did, still, share a meal or two.

Anthea, standing in the concourse with her suitcase, surrounded by strangers, thought: do I really frame my whole existence with the front door opening and closing, and Sunday lunch? Can this really be so?

It was so. She looked across at Jason, chewing, turning the pages of his magazine. She wheeled the case in through the open frontage, and touched his arm.

—We must go.

He nodded, not looking up. Something throbbed tinnily through the iPod.

When she had been young, songs were still full of passion and yearning.

She heard herself say, absurdly:—I have had a vision. An epiphany. From now on—

He nodded again. A security man in epaulettes approached them, speaking on a mobile. He gestured at a rucksack, left in the aisle.

—That yours?

Anthea looked at it.—Jason! Wake up!

He looked up, he came to, he picked up his rucksack and bought his magazine. As they left the shop, and walked towards the platform, invisible fingers brushed the departures board, whirring the little black strips, and everything changed. The significance of this, as they headed for their train, did not pass Anthea by.

Dorothy, Anthea's aunt, was tall and straight and almost eighty. She lived in a plain grey house in a glen, some fifty miles out of the city. The last time they had come here she had met them at the station, and driven them home: to a place which Anthea had visited every year with her parents, when she was small. As she grew up, and grew away, and after she married James—particularly after she married James—the visits were less regular. Still, she had wanted to bring little Jason, though had foolishly underestimated how tiresome the journey might be for both of them. She had packed books and tapes and colouring pens, but Jason wanted only to explore, and shrieked when restrained. She followed his eager progress down the aisles, bumping into things, jogging people carrying cups from the buffet, stepping on and off the place which worked the automatic doors. They stood in the aisle outside their compartment and she held him up to look at flashing fields and cows and distant hills. He squirmed and wriggled; she put him down and he ran into the toilet, slamming the door. She pushed it open quickly, and banged his forehead. He fell on the slippery floor and screamed.

Hours later, she phoned her husband from Dorothy's quiet house.

—How are you? she asked him, sensing preoccupation.

—Tired. She could hear the rustle of paper.—I've got a lot on.

—Well, at least you can do it in peace, she said, hearing Jason, revived from his sleep in the car, revving up along the landing.

—Don't get at me, he said in irritation. —I'd like to be having a break myself.

Anthea swallowed. From the window by the telephone she could see sheep on the hillside, moving up the slope as the sun went down. Upstairs, Jason banged into an unfamiliar door and cried.

—What's happening? Jason demanded. —What's going on?

—Nothing serious, said Anthea.—I'd better go.

She said goodbye and then, hearing Dorothy hasten to the rescue, stood for a moment looking out over the hillside. The thin bleating of the sheep came in at the open window. She used to stand here when she was little, too.

Jason, after a bath, calmed down. She sat on the bed beside him, in the blue and white room where she used to sleep as a child. She told him this, smoothing his damp hair, and he yawned.

—It's nice here. I like it in Scotland.

— Good. She kissed him, and stayed until, a few minutes later, he fell asleep.

Then she went out to join Dorothy, walking round the stone-walled garden, taking the last of the sun.

— Such a pity James couldn't come, said Dorothy, tugging at dead-heads.

— Yes.

Anthea thought of the train journey, and the long car ride afterwards, and how they would have to do it all again in three days' time. She thought how much she would like to be here with a husband who wanted to be here too, just because she was. The evening air was sharp and chill; she pulled her jacket around her, remembering the phone call. — He's got a lot on, she told her aunt. — He said he'd love to have a break.

— Poor man. He must come another time.

The sun sank lower; they went indoors. Anthea showed photographs of Jason's friends at nursery, the birthday party and magician; herself and her husband, watching it all.

— You all look nice and happy, said her aunt, in her lilting voice.

This year, Dorothy was not at the barrier to greet them. She drove, she had said in her letter, only locally these days. Outside the station, Jason and Anthea took a cream and green bus. They rumbled along Princes Street and out of the city, past Arthur's Seat. The sky was beginning to darken, the evening to draw in. They drove through the suburbs, stopping and starting, and out to a country road. Every now and then they passed earthworks, and JCBs at rest, and a notice, planted in the verge: R.D. MACLEAN RISES TO THE CHALLENGE. Anthea rested her head against the glass, as she sometimes did in the library. She watched the weak spring sunlight fade into gathering cloud and, as sometimes in the library, felt herself fading also, as if everything, even her breath, had stopped. She had expected to feel refreshed, restored: instead, she felt emotionally adrift, displaced. As for the moment of epiphany—

—How long till we get there? asked Jason.

It was what he had asked when he was little. She looked at her watch.

—About half an hour?

The landscape became hillier; coarse heather stretched on either side of the road, which began to twist. Sheep moved through the heather, pale and slow.

—Deer, Jason said suddenly.—I can see deer.

—Where? Anthea followed his finger.—Are you sure?

—Certain.

It was certain James would leave her. And then—

Anthea closed her eyes and saw two notices. BEFORE. AFTER. A great moment lay ahead in her life, and what was she going to do with it?

A few drops of rain fell against the window, and the driver switched on the lights. When she looked out again, she could see nothing.

—We'll have to phone Dorothy from the bus stop.

But Dorothy, when they drew into the village, was already there. She got out of her small black car and came to greet them, straight and clear-spoken.

—My dears, my dears—

She kissed them, and looked them up and down. She was wearing a gabardine mac, and her white hair was coiled in a plait round her crown, as it had always been. Her skin was soft and her voice still lilting: she was eighty years old and had lived all her life in the same house, unmarried, teaching, gardening, writing letters and playing the piano. She was liked and respected and now, as she led them back to the car, asking Jason to open the boot for their luggage, Anthea thought: I have known her always. I shall tell her the truth: about my life, my marriage, my failure to —

Jason slammed the boot shut; they got in the car. Dorothy drove slowly out of the village and into the heart of the glen. She asked about the journey, and London, and Jason's school. She told them about the recent storms and how cold it had been, even in April. They came to the gate at the end of the lane, and Jason got out to open it. He stood there, waving them through, lightening up a bit, and they drove slowly up towards the house, where a lamp had been left on for their arrival.

Supper was in the kitchen, where a wood stove burned. A cat lay in a box beside it, on a piece of folded blanket. Jason went over.

— Is this the one you had when we came before?

— Of course. Bertie's been here for ever.

Dorothy moved about the kitchen, putting plates to warm, refusing offers of help after their long journey. Anthea sat at the table, drinking wine, looking at Jason, suddenly softer, nicer. He had picked up the cat and sat down, rubbing his face against dense fur.

— He's lovely.

Newspapers lay in neat piles on chairs, the clock ticked steadily, everything was dusted and clean.

Jason, over supper, said with unusual directness: — It's all very nice here. It all looks cared for.

— Not like his home, you understand, said Anthea.

Dorothy sat straight and tall in the carving chair which had been her father's.

— I'm sure his home is beautiful. — She offered second helpings. — Sometimes I find it a bit much just now, but I try to keep it going. That's so important, don't you think? You must care for things—for every single thing.

Neither of them answered this. They ate well, and went to bed early. Anthea knew she would say nothing.

She woke at daybreak, hearing the birds. A crack of light came through the curtains, and she lay without moving, aware of the deep silence enfolding the house, the silence of the glen. No traffic, no voices, no coming or going: only this song. The light between curtains and ceiling grew paler, the chorus more full and divine. Anthea got out of bed and went to the window.

Dew lay on the grass of Dorothy's garden; the stones of the wall which bordered it shone faintly with moisture; beyond, a mist was rising from the floor of the glen, towards the hillside and the trees. The clouds were dissolving, drifting away; she opened the window and the air was cold and sweet.

She dressed in jeans and sweater. She went out of the bedroom and along the landing. The door to the blue room, where Jason was sleeping, was shut, but Dorothy's was held ajar with a tapestry footstool. Anthea remembered it from her childhood. She stepped past very quietly; Dorothy stirred.

—Hello?

—I'm just going out for a walk.

—Good idea.

She went to the bathroom, then down the shallow staircase, along to the kitchen, taking her jacket from a peg, and out of the unlocked door. The garden was shining and wet; her walking shoes squeaked on the grass. Spring came so late in the north, and the flowerbeds were almost empty, bulbs just appearing in the dark earth. Mist wove in and out of the bare trees on the hillside. There was a burn not far from the garden wall, and Anthea could hear it; she could hear the sheep, bleating here and there above the heather. The gate to the garden was set in the wall, hung with ivy. She pushed it open.

In summer, the glen was thick with fern. Now everything lay low. She walked along a footpath towards the farm where she used to be brought, as a child, to watch the milking. She had brought Jason, too, ten years ago: it had been a highlight. No one was up yet, not even here. A black and white dog on a chain was nosing an empty metal bowl: it scraped on the concrete of the yard and his chain rattled. He stopped at her approach, then began barking wildly, ready to round her up. A door opened in the farmhouse and a man looked out. Anthea walked on, following the footpath, which followed the line of the hill, onwards into the trees.

Here the birdsong was extraordinary: she slowed down, listening, smelling damp earth and leaf mould. Moisture clung to the smooth grey trunks of beech, as it clung to the garden wall; strands of mist hung here and there; there were sounds from somewhere not far away—twigs snapping, footsteps, panting.

She stopped, and stood waiting.

From round a bend in the footpath a young man came running. He wore dark blue shorts and a white singlet; a dark blue sweatshirt was tied round his waist. He ran steadily, breathing hard; he had straight light hair and an angular face, and as he drew nearer she saw the sweat drip down his cheekbones and the sheen of it on his bare limbs. His breath streamed out in clouds on the cold still air before him; he came closer, and she saw that his eyes were a yellowy green like a stone beneath water.

He was looking straight ahead, towards the next curve of the path, but for a moment, as she stepped back to let him pass, their eyes met and they acknowledged one another: she a woman much older, up early, out on her own; a woman who leaned against library windows and felt that her life was over; a woman at a turning point, in crisis — yes, yes, of course that's what she was, not dead but sleeping, asleep all her life and waiting for —

And he, with his yellow-green eyes and sinewy arms, his sweating energy and clouds of breath before him — he looked at her briefly, and gave her a nod and a flickering smile, and then he had passed her, feet pounding the damp earth, gasps growing fainter as he came to the swell of the hillside, rounding it, off through the trees, and gone.

Anthea stood there. The sky above the bare branches was lightening; the birdsong, which she had ceased to be aware of, was rising high towards it. She listened, and then she walked on again, leaving the footpath and climbing the hill, until she was out of the trees and could look down across them, towards the farm, towards Dorothy's house. It stood square and plain and solid: she could see, as the last of the mist dissolved, curtains drawn back and Dorothy at her open bedroom window, leaning out, looking down on her well-tended garden and out towards the glen, where Anthea might be seen.

A singular, well-run life. Her father's sister, unmarried and content.

In the farmyard the dog had been let off his chain. She could see him following the farmer to the field gate at the back, where black and white cows were waiting. The gate swung open, the cows filed through towards the milking parlour. After a while, the hum of the machine began.

She walked slowly down the hillside. The mist had risen, the sun was coming up, it was still cold but she did not feel it. She came to the trees again, to the footpath;

she drew a deep breath, raising her arms above her head, and then she was running, running, running.

Five People Waiting

THERE THEY STOOD in the rain.

—Let's get this straight. Derek lives in the garage, and Mel in the mobile home.

—Correct.

—And Tonya—he peered at Eddie's clipboard—Ms Tonya Magee, that is, she lives in the house.

—Which she owns. Likewise the land, the garage, and the wreck of a caravan which you see before you.

One of the (few) things Dave liked about this job was the way Eddie talked. Put things. He could have gone far, Eddie, if he'd had a mind to.

—And the issues are . . .

He liked the way he said issues. At school he'd spent half his time in a dream, couldn't make out a half of it, but he'd grown up in this job, had more of a command of language, sort of thing. Not up to Eddie's standard, but getting there.

—Benefit fraud, said Eddie, shielding his clipboard from the rain as best he could. —We're talking years. Occupation of a mobile home without the owner's consent. She wants him out. She wants them both out.

—And Derek's the brother? Tricky.

—Derek's the brother, but Mel is the problem. An ex to whom she misguidedly gave a home. That thing.

They stood and surveyed the scene. The caravan sat rotting contentedly in a bed of lush grass. A hen was

sheltering beneath the steps and a cheerful puff of smoke
rose from a stovepipe chimney. Dave pictured a snug,
illegal little woodburner, a terrier crashed out before it
and Mel stirring his tea. Independence, that was the thing.
Somewhere to call your own.

— Right, then. We'd better crack on. Set to with a
will, as you might say.

— Gird up our loins, suggested Dave.

Eddie ignored this. He liked to be The One. And he
pushed open the rusting five-barred gate and strode pur-
posefully through. Dave followed. As per. Across at the
house a window opened and a fat blonde figure leaned
out in the wet. Then she was opening the front door and
they strode up, and stood before her.

Blimmineck.

Ms Tonya Magee, a woman well into her forties, was
wearing white shorts, high-heeled white mules and a
shocking pink strappy top thing which — He swallowed.

Eddie was ticking things off on his clipboard. Name.
Address. Names of so-called tenants.

— You don't need to bother with Derek, said Ms
Magee. — Not today. It's him I want rid of.

She jerked her head towards the cheerful chimney.
Mingled in with the woodsmoke there came across the
yard an unmistakeable smell of another kind of smoke
altogether: something which Dave was familiar with from
quiet evenings at home on his own. He had to open all
the windows before his mum came back. Burn a bit of
incense. Sandalwood. Could pass for soap. Just.

— Ooh, love, whatever is that funny smell? You been
having a bath?

— Right, then, said Eddie.

They strode past the garage, all shut up and silent, the
rain drumming on the roof. A filthy curtain hung at a

grimy window. Imagine. Living in a garage. When he told his mum about some of the things that went on she could only shake her head.

The caravan steps were rotting. Eddie stood gingerly upon them. He knocked on the door. Not a dicky bird. He knocked again. Not a peep.

—Mr Young! This is the Council! Open up!

Silence. Perhaps Mr Mel Young, forty-three years of age and unemployed for the duration, really had gone out. Perhaps he was laughing at them from behind a hedge. Dave looked over his shoulder, saw only rain, neglected acres, rusty stuff.

—Mr Young!

The door was opened abruptly. Something fell off it. Effing and blinding followed.

—Do you mind, said Eddie.

Mel Young was a sight and a half. Wasted or what? To think that he and Tonya Magee had once—Ugh. Dave, who wanted a girlfriend more than anything in the world, took it all in. He saw the little woodburner, stuff heaped everywhere, a hen. He saw his mother's face.

—On the bed? A hen on the bed?

—Mr Young. Eddie tapped his clipboard.—I think you know why we're here. I'm serving you with a Warning.

Now it was really chucking it down. Dave stood at the foot of the steps and turned his collar up. He felt like an old donkey left out in a field. Twenty-eight, and he felt like a donkey. How sad was that?

—You are required by law to quit these premises within two weeks. Failure to do so will result in arrest and the arrival of the bailiffs.

Mel gave a hollow laugh. Dave had a vision of the hen (a Rhode Island Red) being tucked beneath a burly arm and taken away, squawking, until such time as Mel Young could afford to get her back again. Poor old thing.

Eddie held out the Warning. Mel Young folded his arms. Eddie sent it spinning into the caravan and came down the steps. The door slammed behind him. Rain flew about.

They went back to the house.

—Well? asked Tonya Magee.

—I have served Mr Young with Papers, said Eddie. He sounded like a hanging judge.

—Suppose it's a start. Fancy a cuppa? she asked.

Dave thought: She will make us a piping hot pot of tea and when Eddie goes to the toilet she'll ask if I'd like to come back on my own. He could see them, upstairs on a quilt, a lamp with a tarty pink shade shining through the rainy light, and she showing him how it was done. Exactly how.

—No, thanks, said Eddie. —We'd better be on our way. We'll be in touch.

—That's nice. She gave him a meaningful little smile.

They trudged back to the van and drove on to the next job, two miles away along the main road, through the swishing rain. Dave lit a cig and sat smoking. He watched the wipers going back and forth, back and forth: in perfect harmony, as Eddie might have put it, and never ever meeting.

Days

A T A QUARTER to eight, rather later than he thought was right, Spencer, still in his dressing gown, felt his way down the dark narrow stairs, and through to the kitchen. May morning light: the curtains had been drawn back, the range made up; he could hear the kettle, warming upon it. Jem, out of bed half an hour ago, had got everything started and set off for her walk, and what was left for him to do?

He went slowly across to the table: this, too, had been laid, though he had asked her—specifically asked her—to leave it to him. He made out Thea's cups—which, yes, he might drop if he weren't careful, but he was more than careful—set, bright and angular, against the comfortable curve of the teapot; he laid his hands on plate and knife at each place. She had not put out the bread: he would do that.

He was doing it as the door to the street opened, and Jem returned. The grandfather clock struck eight as she crossed the hall. Just as the chime of the church clock came from the end of the village. He could hear her pulling her boots off.

—I've brought the paper. She dropped it by her plate.

—I asked you to leave the table to me.

—Sorry. I wasn't thinking.

He sat down, felt for the bread knife. The lid of the kettle began to clatter.

—How was your walk?

—The heron was there, said Jem, taking the teapot over, making the tea.

—Was he now? Spencer let the first thick crumbling slice fall on to the breadboard and closed his eyes, picturing the waving reeds, the river, the still grey silhouette. They had known that bird for years.

—And I saw Thea on the way back. Jem returned, set the teapot between them, pulled out her chair.—She's going to call in before the concert: I said we could all walk up together.

—How is she?

—She said she hadn't slept. Do you want me to finish slicing that loaf?

—I do not. What's in the paper?

She sat down, shook it out, read him the headlines while the tea brewed. Plans for the Silver Jubilee: a party in the village. Parties everywhere, though everyone knew the king was frail and failing.

—He's done his threescore years and ten, said Spencer, spooning on marmalade and missing.—Mary, of course, will go on for ever.

This autumn—on 11th October, 1935—he himself would be sixty-nine. His life's work was upstairs in the studio, all through the house, hanging on walls all over the country. But not in a London gallery, not any more. Locally, of course, he still showed, along with everyone else, but only old unsold work, which mostly remained unsold. Who had money at the moment, anyway? In their rented houses, they were all just getting by.

—Another cup?

—No, thanks.

He leaned back in the Windsor chair and closed his eyes. Children ran past on their way to school. Their quick light footsteps and high voices lifted his heart.

After breakfast, companionable enough in the end, with a letter from Nina in London, came, always, the most difficult question of the day. What to do with it. Jem had gone up to the studio, was settling down. This evening was the concert—recital—in the church. Between now and then—Spencer stood in the middle of the room. If anyone in the past had asked him—as occasionally an interviewer had asked—What is your routine? he would have been able to tell them almost without thinking. At work the moment breakfast was over: up in the studio or out with his easel, tramping over fields, through copse and spinney, looking, looking. Now—

Jem came down mid-morning, to see how he was getting on. He was getting nowhere, still in his dressing-gown, just sitting.

—This won't do.

—Can't seem to start a bloody thing.

—Come on up. Come and be with me.

He climbed the stairs, went to the bedroom and slowly dressed. Then he walked along the landing, touching the sill of the tall sash window which overlooked the garden and had become a stage post. He touched the chest where he knew Jem would have stood a jug of flowers, and felt for them, and smelled syringa and lilac. Along to the studio, whose door she had left open. He touched the frame.

—One day I'll just fall right through here.

—Please don't.

She was, he could tell from her voice, bent over the press, her back to him.

He made out its bulk, a huge dark thing, and something lighter in front of it, which was Jem. He found the rush-bottomed chair, knocking a pile of magazines off the window sill on the way: all those back numbers of *Studio*, which had now and then featured his work, and *The Woodcut*, which featured Jem's, along with Gill, Ravilious, Gertrude Hermes, all that lot.

—Bugger.

—Leave them.

He left them, stepping awkwardly round the heap, sinking into his chair at last.

—What are you up to?

—Still on the almanac. I'm in August now: end of the harvest.

—Lovely.

He heard the arm of the press descend, and closed his eyes, seeing within him the stretch of stubble, the fleeing hare, the scythe. He knew just how she would do it, how August, in black and white, would still burn on the page. They had shown each other their work for so many years: he the painter, now and then making prints; she the wood engraver and cutter—bookplates, diaries and almanacs, decorations, illustrations. Now and then she ventured into watercolour—beautiful things. Spencer Watkins and Jemima Hutchinson: for years they had shown, talked, overlapped, hung, and no day was long enough—no good day, anyway—for everything they had to do and say. Now it was only her. Did she mind, in her heart, that she could no longer show him, ask him, try again? If so, she never said it.

—Oh, bloody hell.

—Now what?

—Nothing.

He opened his eyes again, travelled the room: the press,

the two tall windows, the canvasses stacked all along the wall—these shapes he could distinguish. That was it. He could not see the books on the other window sill, nor his paintings on the walls, even though this was the lightest room in the house and his colours had always been so strong. Not a bloody thing.

Birds called from the garden, and a fly buzzed about. Was the flypaper still up?

Perhaps it was a bee—he wouldn't want a bee to get stuck. He listened intently: no, a fly. That was what everyone said: that your hearing became more acute, would help to compensate. They also said he should learn Braille, that with his painter's sensitivity he'd master it in no time.

The fly buzzed, the arm of the press came down again, and a breeze shook the window pane. Outside, the garden stretched to the stream, and beyond stretched the fields of Essex, and the river, the River Pant, bordered by willows and osiers and reeds: all of which, with the heron, the coot and moorhen and wild duck, they had rejoiced in when they arrived from London. They had walked for miles, Nina on piggyback when she grew tired, across the fields, along the river, through the villages: Wimbish Green, Debden, Blackmore End, Beazley End, Black Nolley. Thirty miles east lay Constable country: once, on a walk, thinking about those monumental landscapes, those tumbling clouds in the skies over Hampstead Heath, he had for a moment seen a tow-haired boy in a rust-coloured jacket bent gulping over a stream, seen him as clearly as his own hand; said to Jem—Look! Constable's boy! Then the lad—playing truant?—had scrambled up from the bank and run off, and Spencer saw he was dark, with a white school shirt, and nothing like his vision. But still—for a moment he had lived within a painting, which was what, all his life, he had ever wanted to do.

A mile or so along the river from here a stone bridge (beneath which Nina had loved to watch the watery light reflected) led west to the village and east to a long straight road to Castle Wickham. It was bordered by rustling poplars, silver-green in the sun. He painted there in the summer of 1925, found himself thinking all the time of France, where there were many such roads, and where he and Jem had spent summers after the war, visiting the Paris studios, failing to find the grave of his nephew, Captain Anthony Watkins, killed at Verdun.

Spencer himself, already middle-aged, had spent the war in Palestine, leaving Jem and baby Nina in their rented flat in Camden, while he served as Official War Artist in the Royal Army Medical Corps. En route, briefly posted to Salonika, he had run into Stanley Spencer, serving in the same regiment with one or two others from the Slade—a different generation. They shared a cigarette in a rundown café, talked a bit, made the obvious remark about their names.

—But everybody calls me Cookham, said young Stanley Spencer, pulling out a little book from his pocket. He showed it: a Gowans and Gray volume of *Old Masters*.—Masaccio and Giotto, Fra Angelico, they're the only ones who matter to me.

Soon afterwards, he was posted to Macedonia.

Years later, on a December afternoon, Spencer Watkins, returned from the war and struggling to make a living, went to the National War Paintings Exhibition at the National Gallery and found himself in front of Stanley Spencer's *Travoys Arriving with Wounded at a Dressing Station at Smol, Macedonia*, 1919. If anyone had come up to him then, he would not have been able to speak. Later, back in the freezing flat, he tried to write about it—about the picture's extraordinary combination of drama and stillness; the way everything was seen from behind: how the great dark mules (those ears, that enquiring turn of a head) thrust deep into the picture plane, gazing, like the Red Cross medics accompanying the wounded, at the luminous space of an operating theatre. It was as if everyone were moving towards a lamplit altar, the army blankets covering the wounded men billowing like the cloth of heaven. A Giotto for our times, he wrote, and then there came the sound of the key in the lock, and Jem and Nina were home.

—Spencer? What are you thinking about? She was laying out prints to dry; he could hear the soft murmur of air as each sheet fell on to the table.

He tried to remember.

—The war, he said at last.—Stanley Spencer.

—The war, said Jem.—How did you get there?

—By way of Constable. Or something. Never mind. It feels like lunchtime.

—Are you all right?

He said:—I am a conduit. That is what an artist is. Without my work I am but a hollow reed.

—You sound like an Old Testament prophet.

— That is how I feel.

—Like a prophet?

—Like a broken reed.

Thea, unable to contain herself, arrived at lunchtime, smelling of clay and exuding an air of anguish. She tapped out a cigarette; Spencer sensed that her fingers were trembling.

—Not a good day?

—It's hell. Hellish. She inhaled to the depths. — He

wants us all to get *on*. He wants it all to be like the old college days, and it can't be. It *can't*.

Spencer was sympathetic, but also detected something of the theatrical. Thea had always needed an audience — for a potter she was an extraordinary extrovert: like her work, of course, which had given her a name. Mind you, beside Diana, for whom John Ebbe was abandoning her at last, Thea was a minor player.

He listened, and half-listened, as smoke drifted over the table and Jem made lunch. Diana had a fall of dark hair pinned up with an insouciant clip. Big-breasted, with a fabulous bottom. She wore lipstick the colour of a peony, but only in the evenings, so you longed for the moment to come. Her work: strong bold paintings, almost abstract, quite unlike the work of any woman he knew. That laugh, that look: just for you.

—Spencer!

Irresistible. He had resisted, because by the time they came down here, all in ones and twos, he was long married to Jem, and both believed profoundly in the vows and values of marriage. And even if he had never failed to notice Diana, and had allowed himself, now and then, to dream, things were different now. Everything was different.

He could remember, but not properly see her, just as he could barely see Thea, talking still, across the table. He knew her rust-gold curls, springing from a tightly bound bandana; knew her pale freckled skin and greenish eyes; her long fingers, caked with clay. He had known her ever since, a different generation, she and John came down to live in the village, settled in, seemed so happy — until Diana's arrival, leaving a marriage behind her. And a child, apparently. He had observed Thea age a little, but could not see what Jem described as John began to leave her:

the sudden lines, the pallor. When Thea, in calmer days, came into a room, you noticed, and thought you would like to get to know her. When Diana entered, you fell. He had almost fallen.

Jem served sorrel soup, fresh bread, the last of the mousetrap, the first garden lettuce.

— That rabbit.

— I'd pot him if I could, said Spencer, raising his spoon to his lips.

— How are you, Spencer? asked Thea, whose crisis had obliterated all other conversation between them for weeks. — How goes it?

— It goes nowhere, said Spencer, as soup fell on his shirt. — Never mind. I'm looking forward to this evening. Old Baldicoot's nephew.

— Niece, said Jem, who had designed the pro-gramme. — Niece and fiancé. Brahms and Schubert sonatas.

— Lovely.

— And Britten.

— Ah.

In the afternoon, Jem went back to the studio, Thea to the pottery — where they knew she would pace about, smoking — and he out to the garden. It was really warm now; he stood breathing it all in, went slowly down the path with his stick and poked about a bit. He felt the watercress clumping up by the stream. For the millionth time he tried to tell himself: You have done a great deal. Your work is here and no one can take that away. Be glad. No matter how many times he tried to say this, nothing could quell his loss and need.

He felt stones underfoot on the path and kicked them: serve them bloody right. Then he found his chair, and sat in the sun, as the old are supposed to do; he fell asleep and woke in need of tea, which Jem brought out, and which they shared, talking of this and that. Garden things. Jem did a bit of snipping.

In the evening they set off to the church. Spencer wore his old linen jacket, and Panama hat.

—How do I look? he asked Jem in the hall.

—Very handsome. As always. And I?

—What are you wearing?

—The rose-print frock and faded rose jacket.

—Gorgeous. And you smell gorgeous.

Thea tapped on the door and came in as they kissed.

—Oh. Sorry.

—Nothing to be sorry for.

—I must be driving you mad, coming over all the time.

—Never.

—And you look lovely, said Jem, admiring the green and black, the beads.

As they left the house Spencer gave them each an arm. They walked up the street in the slanting evening sun; he began to sing.

—*Doing the Lambeth Walk* . . .

People were walking up alongside. They greeted one another, and he recognised every voice: the women from Jem's WI class; Peter Gillespie; one or two old boys from the British Legion; Miss Lawrence from the school. Caroline and Tilly, holding her mother's hand. Eight years old in a summer frock and sandals: he had painted her when she was three.

—Of course I know it's you.

Old Baldicoot was waiting at the door, his cassock such a bright white thing.

—So good of you to come.

—We're looking forward to it.

Music on a summer evening. Inside the church, he sat imagining the shafts of light, the dust, the stained glass colours falling on to stone. Patches of purple and crimson, indigo and gold, suddenly splashed on a shoe, as people came quietly in and settled down. He heard the coughs, the murmured greetings, the rustle of Jem's programmes.

—Are they here? he asked her in an undertone.

—Yes. She said it quickly, quietly, mindful as he was of Thea beside him, stiff with tension.

—Where?

—Up at the front.

And he tried to picture them, on their first public outing, John Ebbe and Diana Devas, defiantly in love. Ebbe was a man women fell for, over and over again: tall and dark, crumpled and vague, with a fleeting smile. He had the air of one to whom things happened—not a strider, not a go-getter—but he got, you noticed, every-thing he wanted: the Cork Street gallery, admiring notices, distinctive women, from each of whom, every few years, he quietly moved.

Heavy footsteps came down the aisle, and people qui-etened. Old Baldicoot began to burble on. Then, with a burst of welcoming applause, the two young musicians came out from the vestry and took their places. That marvellous moment of tuning up, everyone hushed and expectant. Then it began.

The first notes sounded, clear as water.

He thought: This is what it means to be alive. In death there is none of this.

It was a thought he could share with no one, not even Jem. In the past, he would have tried to show it in his work. And he closed his eyes on the shapes he could not see—the dark raised lid of the piano, the lifted violin—and as the music soared and fell he thought of his paintings, which Roger Fry had once said were so vibrant and strong, and showed he had learned from Matisse. Fry had been an old prune—but still: those remarks had helped launch his career. Then he thought of his last print, something quite different, made in the autumn two years ago: Hill Farm, with the ploughed land rising, striped and severe, behind that square of windowed stone. His paintings were loose, extravagant, even; in his prints he sought discipline, flatness, formality. Hill Farm had sold over and over again.

Something was happening. Thea, beside him, was weeping silently, and her body shook. He put his arm around her, drew her close.

Afterwards, it was all quite jolly: the village hall, doors flung wide to the evening sun, trestle tables, drinks and a WI buffet—a try-out for the Jubilee, perhaps. And packed to the gills, though after a while people took their plates out on to the grass. Thea—how he admired her—splashed her face in the basin of the WC and braved it out, talking to everyone, studiedly—he knew—turned away from Ebbe and Diana. He turned away, too, once Jem had told him where they were, wondering if in fact there was anyone there prepared to give them a word. What would Old Baldicoot make of it? Adulterers under his nose, brazenly coming into the church, even if its use this evening was entirely secular. Probably, Spencer thought, now on his second large glass, he hadn't twigged. Not as if any of them were exactly regular attenders. And anyway, tonight was proud-uncle night, the three of them circulating, modestly accepting compliments, happy.

Jem was surrounded by her class. He talked to

Caroline, made Tilly laugh; talked to Peter Gillespie, whose work he'd always liked; suddenly found himself alone, and then a tall figure was in front of him, and Ebbe was saying, in that maddening upper-class voice:

—Spencer. It's me, John.

—Of course I know it's you.

—How are you?

—Much as usual.

—Can I get you another drink?

—No, thanks. He knocked back the last of the glass. — Well, now, what have you got to say for yourself?

Ebbe coughed, hesitated. — Only—well, just hoping we'll see you and Jem again soon. Diana and I—we're awfully fond of you both.

—We're fond of you. But Thea—he wished he could look round the crowded hall, see where she was—She's distraught. It won't do, John, really it won't.

—Well, I—of course I'm sorry about it all, it's been very upsetting—

—For Thea.

John put his hand on his arm. Spencer shook it off.

—We just hope that in time—

—Oh, time, said Spencer, his earlier party mood quite gone. — We're all supposed to get used to everything in time. He looked around him, saw blur after blurry shape, heard Diana laugh. — Where's Jem?

—I'll fetch her for you, said John, as if that made up for everything, and was gone.

He stood alone in the sea of people, adrift and old.

They talked it all over in bed. Both of them knew, despite Spencer's earlier irritation, that as the months went by the waters would probably close, that by Christmas they'd all be in and out of each other's houses again.

—And after all, said Jem, yawning, —Thea might meet someone else.

—Who? Who else could she possibly meet here?

—What about Peter Gillespie?

—He's a pansy.

—Are you sure?

—Certain.

—Oh, well, said Jem, blowing the lamp out, —I can't think about it any more now.

They lay holding hands in the smoky darkness. Then Jem yawned again, gave him a kiss, turned over. Within moments, he knew she was asleep.

He lay awake, listening to the stream.

Dedicated to the artist Jane Tuely

For Life

THERE WERE SOME pretty peculiar people at Jenny's funeral. So thought Persephone, pouring herself a drink that evening in her square flint cottage, watching the rain tip down. The phone rang. That would be Henry.

— How was it?

She settled herself in the wing chair. Where to begin? As she drew a breath she saw again that dippy Stop/Go boy in the lane on the way home, holding up the traffic for a flock of sheep. They bounced past the car, the farmer in front and the dog behind them and she knew, as she waited, and the rain began, that Henry would be ringing, and ringing again.

— How are you? she asked him.

— Dreadful. That heavy sigh. Henry had always been a sigher. She took another sip from the cut-glass tumbler. — Dreadful, he said again. — Tell me everything. Was it packed?

— Pretty full.

— She should have had a cathedral. Go on.

— The village was there. Pretty well everyone. Her friends from the school. The niece, who arranged it all.

— What's she like?

— I hardly spoke to her. Then Dr Dickson, the Marie Curie people, Mrs Burton — she'll be bereft, she was in every day. Still feeding the cat, I gather.

— That poor cat, said Henry brokenly. — Can't you take her in?

— No, said Persephone. Then she went on, — There were a few oddities.

She could feel him stiffen.

— Oddities? Men?

— A Dutch boy. Lanky, very pale. Specs.

— Dutch? How do you know?

— I spoke to him, Henry.

— At the graveside?

— Of course not. At the reception.

But it had been at the sunlit graveside that she had noticed him, a stranger amongst all the familiar faces, awkward and ashen. There was also a plain plump woman in a bright pink anorak. Thin hair and blotchy skin. Where had she come from? Those closest to Jenny (excluding poor Henry) — Mrs Burton, her colleagues, all the old friends made over twenty years of living in the village, Persephone herself — had kept a respectful distance as the coffin was lowered down past the bright sheets of artificial grass on to the waiting earth. Somehow those two were up at the front: she noticed them as she raised her head — his pallor, her dreadful pink.

Then the vicar — someone else who had been very fond of Jenny — spoke the lines which were all most people nowadays knew of the Anglican liturgy. Ashes to ashes, dust to dust, and the funeral director stepped respectfully forward and threw in a handful of earth. The vicar invited the mourners to throw in their own tokens of remembrance, and a little shower — sprigs of rosemary, posies from cottage gardens — pattered down. Persephone did not approve of this: she liked things to be simple and austere, and — unbeliever though she was — to follow the ancient traditions of the church. A handful of earth, and no more. Either that, or keep right away from it, burn in the city crematorium, and no pretending.

—Hello? said Henry.—Are you still there? Who was the Dutchman?

—I talked to him afterwards, in the village hall. And the woman in pink.

—What woman? For God's sake, Persephone.

—Sorry. It's been a long day. Let me get another drink.

She got up and went to the decanter. The rain had eased off, but you could tell it was only temporary. Not a soul about, the cottages round the Green showing the flicker of the television, everyone recovering, catching up with Wimbledon. She returned to her chair.

—Now then.

And she described it all: the hymns, *The Lord is My Shepherd; Immortal, Invisible*—Her favourite, said Henry, his voice breaking; the address—It could never do her justice, he said; the long slow procession beneath the yew—I should have been there. Oh, God. And then?

——Then we all went back to the village hall, as I said. It was still sunny at that point, so the doors were open, that was very nice, and well, you know, white wine or elderflower, sandwiches done by Mrs B. and one or two cricket wives, all very good, and everyone began to unwind. It had all been pretty emotional—

—Of course it had. Of course. It must have been hell.

—Well, I wouldn't quite say—

—It was hell for me, said Henry.

—Of course it was, she said quietly.

—Imagining it all. Stuck in that bloody court.

—Did you win?

—No. A wasted day, when I should have been—Hang on a minute.

There were sounds in the background; she heard him open the study door.

—Shan't be long, he called out, and then he was back again.—Supper. Go on. Cut to the chase.

—What chase?

—The Dutchman. For God's sake, Persephone, he said again.

—He was just a boy, she said.—A student, I think. He'd met her at some kind of singing thing. Or encounter thing. I couldn't quite make it out.

—Encounter? That doesn't sound like Jenny.

—I know. And there was someone else—an awful bright woman, who came over to join us.

Persephone, whose height and general bearing could make her, she knew, appear intimidating, had grown used down the years to new people avoiding her at social gatherings, or approaching with some diffidence. The Dutch boy—Johann—had been shy and monosyllabic when she asked how he came to be here; the blotchy pink person had smiled uncertainly. There was nothing diffident about the woman who made her way through the crowd and extended—almost flung out—her hand.

—Hi! I'm Elizabeth.

—How do you do? Persephone took the hand and released it.

—And you must be Persephone.

Elizabeth, on the face of it an attractive woman—dark wavy hair clipped on either side with tortoiseshell, Liberty summer frock—smiled with irritating openness.

Persephone gazed down at her.

—How do you know that?

—I thought it must be you. I saw you talking to these two—Elizabeth flashed a smile at Johann and Pink—and thought I must come over. Jenny talked about you often.

—Did she? asked Persephone, by now quite disconcerted.

—She was such a special person. We only got to know her quite recently.

—You all know each other?

Johann nodded, and shifted about.

—That's right, said Large Pink.

—I'm sorry, I didn't catch your name. Persephone inclined towards her.

—I'm Margaret. Well, Maggie. And she gave a self-deprecating little laugh.

—And you all met Jenny—

—At a workshop, said Maggie.

—A workshop, yes, said Johann.—We sing, we extend our vocal range, he added quietly.

—We get to know each other, Elizabeth told them. She turned back to Persephone.—Do you know about Music for Life?

—I'm afraid I don't.

And then Caroline Crowther came up, and she turned away with relief.

—Do excuse me.

—Music for Life? Henry said now.—What the hell is that?

Renewed domestic sounds came down the line: a knocking, an impatient cry.

—I must go, he said bleakly.—I'll phone you tomorrow.

And he was gone.

Persephone replaced the receiver and topped up her drink; she stood looking out of the window. The sky above the Green had darkened to a vile yellow-grey. She turned on the television. Federer smashed a ball across the net to a roar of applause.

Perhaps it was the whisky. No doubt it was the sad strange day. Persephone, though she fell asleep almost at once, woke in the middle of the night and could not get back to sleep. As every night — it happens to everyone, at a certain age — she stumbled to the bathroom. Then she came back to bed, curled her arms around the pillow and waited for the comfort of oblivion. It did not come. After a while she gave up, and lay in the darkness, thinking everything over: the cars outside the church, so many; the muted greetings as they all walked up the path; the service, with the great absence at its heart, despite the pale oak coffin with its flowers; the long procession to the waiting grave; that pattering of posies, and the sudden realisation that there were people in the crowd she'd never seen before. Who were they, that strange, unsettling trio, who spoke so warmly of Jenny, who had never mentioned them?

Poor Jenny. Poor vibrant Jenny. Persephone had thought in this way for so many weeks, but always in the hope or knowledge that she would see her soon. Speak to her, at least. Towards the end even that had not been possible: the tired voice grew tireder; the Marie Curie nurses picked up the phone. Jenny was comfortable, not to worry, but perhaps not quite up to a visit today. Of course she would give her your love: thanks ever so much.

Now she was gone.

Persephone lay there, seeing before her Jenny in the old days, Jenny as her old self: fair-haired and laughing, coming down the garden path to her car, driving off to her teaching with a wave or a hoot if she saw you; working in the garden at the end of the day, the cat nearby; playing the piano every evening she was alone, Brahms or Chopin drifting out of the window on a summer evening. Inviting you for drinks, for supper, for a Sunday lunch party after church, where she sang in the choir, to a dwindling congregation.

– Come in! How lovely to see you!

They had been close, but — even with the secret they eventually shared — not that close: Persephone was not that close to anyone. And Jenny was convivial, welcoming, but good — so it seemed — at being alone. She had been married, but that was a long time ago, before she moved here, and was rarely spoken of.

Persephone had never married, and in her retirement cherished her independence, her being beholden to no one. She cherished her flint cottage, once a weekend retreat from London and now her home, with her books, antiques and watercolours; she loved the log fire, lit almost every evening; the view of the Green to the front and the rolling hills from the back, where she walked extensively.

Being single is an art. It is, like a marriage, something to work at. Persephone, who had worked hard all her life — terrifying, she knew it, her junior colleagues in the Department of Work & Pensions, respected by her peers — had long since mastered this art, which required, like any other, discipline and routine. The flash of inspiration, the sudden triumphant solving of a problem — these were things which belonged more to her working days than to the single woman living in retirement, but still there were occasional epiphanies, and hers, perhaps, had come with meeting Jenny.

She was not alone in this: lots of people felt better for Jenny's company, and she, of all Persephone's friends, had — apparently — managed the single life better than anyone. Jenny didn't seem single: how did she manage that? Partly it was because she was still working — out there, with colleagues and concerts; partly because of that long-ago marriage, whose ending had not left her embittered but with the air of a woman who knew how to live with someone, should she ever choose to. Mostly, quite simply, it was because of her warmth. She was pretty — good bones, that soft fair hair, those blue-grey eyes; she wore pretty clothes, chic little boutique numbers — a loose-knitted green cardi with a single wooden button, nifty and expensive pumps — quite different from the usual village garb of M&S or Lo-Cost T-shirts, or Persephone's own stylish but muted greys. But that smile, that laugh, that lilting and expressive voice — Come in, how are you, I've had a hideous day, I'm so glad to see you! She made you feel special and needed and loved. Yes, that.

And that, of course, was why Henry had fallen. Thereafter, of course, Jenny had not been entirely single, though miraculously few people were aware of this.

— Oh, dear, Persephone heard herself say aloud into the darkness, and then —

Oh, God.

How quiet it was. Not an owl, not a stirring of the trees on the hill, not a patter of the rain which had subsumed the evening. And Persephone, lying there in her comfortable bed, unshared with anyone, ever, looked at her luminous little clock, saw it was after three, and knew that this hour held Jenny's silence. Perhaps it had been the hour of her death. Whether or not this was so, she was gone, and that was the end of it. If her spirit was anywhere, now — and Persephone, unbeliever to her bones, did not think it was — its manifestation in life would never be here again. No laugh, no hug, no smile meant just for you.

Shored up against loneliness almost all her life, Persephone felt a shiver of it now, a feeling so unfamiliar, and so unpleasant, that the stillness of the night became unbearable, and she reached out, switched the light on, sat up against the pillows. That was better. But poor Jenny, now in eternal darkness.

Was that where she was?

And poor, poor Henry, who had loved her from the moment he saw her, coming down with Phyllis for the weekend, helping with the drinks on Saturday evening—My cousin and his wife are staying, do come and join us—handing a glass to Jenny, and stopping in his tracks. Persephone, not given to observing the nuances of other people's social interactions, had seen it as clearly as sunlight after rain, and stopped in her own tracks, feeling—oh! such a confusion: shock, and anxiety, and something else she could not identify or understand, but which left her, for a moment, on the brink of burning tears.

In the night's deep quiet now, she heard the soft tick of the clock. On and on it went—I am here, I am here. But Jenny's great absence hung over everything, and if she felt it, here in her lamplit bedroom, what must Henry feel?

She pictured him, lying awake beside the sleeping Phyllis, his mind full of Jenny, but with memories much more intimate than Persephone's: pleading letters, secret phone calls; at last her consent, and the rare weekends together, Here. He had based himself here, telling large plain Phyllis that he was helping Persephone with logs, loose tiles, rotting window frames. And she, Persephone, who had never needed help, who could organise roofers, decorators, deliveries of logs, as she had organised and run a whole department, who never lied and did not approve (at all) of clandestine affairs—she had connived in this. Dreadful. Shocking. But blood, it did seem, was thicker than water.

—We're in love, said Henry, and never had she heard

him say such words, nor seen him look so happy. Joy and longing filled his square frame, his open, ordinary face. Even his thinning hair looked thicker. — I don't like to ask, but please, Persephone. Help us.

And Persephone, for the sake of their long-distant childhood, two only-children flung together during the summer holidays, nothing much in common but making the best of it, had said that she would. If Phyllis were to phone, she would cover for him. He could, if he wanted, phone home from here. Of course, he and Jenny could have gone away together, found some nice little hideaway hotel, but—

— I love her house, said Henry. — It feels like home. I love to hear her play. I love the cat. But most of all—

— You love her.

— I can be myself, he said simply, and that was what had done it.

She thought of the boy he had been, always trying to please, to be a good scholar, good player, good son; later a good solicitor, husband, father, when all the time you wondered—as he passed, but without distinction, all exams; as he dropped a ball, or a plate on the kitchen floor, as he came out of the church from his wedding to large plain Phyllis, blinking into the sun— but who is he really? What really makes Henry tick? Is he just a bit dull, or has he—even at fifty, she had wondered this—never quite found his feet?

— Very well, she had said, seeing him alight in every fibre, filled with energy and purpose. — Very well.

The clock ticked into the silence, but more faintly. Persephone had closed her eyes, and now she reached out and turned the lamp off. Finally, she fell asleep.

The morning brought the milk, the paper. The post, in

the country, came much later, sometimes not until after lunch, but she had grown used to this. And oh, the blessed relief of ordinary things, she thought over her breakfast, skimming the headlines, munching her toast, while the radio burbled away. She lost herself in Afghanistan, in—rather differently—Wimbledon, while John Humphreys grilled David Cameron. In the old days, the old full working days, she would no doubt have met Cameron, most certainly would have worked with his PPS. Now she was content to follow things at a distance, just like anyone else.

At the height of her powers, Persephone had not felt like anyone else. Unlike Henry, she had always known what she wanted to do. She had wanted to run things, and to serve a social purpose. This did not make for levity as she grew up, though later her dry humour found appreciation amongst her good colleagues, even as it devastated those less capable. Clever, and more than capable, she had had by anyone's lights a good, even brilliant career, with frankly little time for much outside it. Hence her only intermittent visits to her parents, though she always went for Christmas; hence the rare sightings of her only cousin: perhaps a drink or the theatre if he and Phyllis came up to town, which wasn't often. Family life claimed them, life in Shropshire claimed them; life, as it does, went on.

—I am not, said Persephone aloud, going to think about Henry all day.

She was tired, her head felt thick with tiredness. It was not only the broken night, but all that had led up to it: the shock of Jenny's news, delivered so lightly—I've got a diagnosis at last—but with such sickening effect; her rallying with the treatment, going away for weekends (where? Persephone asked herself now); then her pitiful decline. Henry's visits, coming here afterwards to slump in a chair,

all the heart gone out of him; her own distress. All that.
Too much, too much. Today she would spend quietly,
potter about in the garden, now the rain had blown away,
go for a long walk this afternoon, have an early night.

The phone rang.

—It's me, said Henry.—I'm coming down.

So now she must make up the bed in the guest room;
she must go into town to the butcher. The herb-garden
omelette she would have been happy with this evening
would not do for Henry: not after that long drive, not
in his dreadful state. She must shop, she must cook, she
must comfort.

—I'm exhausted, she said aloud.

Upstairs, she took fresh linen from the airing cupboard,
and made up Henry's single bed. She cut a few roses in
the garden, and put them on his chest of drawers. She
left the window open to air the room and the scent of
the countryside blew in, mingling with the roses: sheep,
rain-soaked grass, manure from the farm, her own flowery
garden. All this might help to restore him: an open
window always offered hope.

Then she went out to the car, raising a hand to old
Burton, working across the Green in his vegetable patch,
and drove away, passing Jenny's empty cottage. She had
passed it before, in the days after her death, it was impossible to get to town without doing so, but now that the
funeral had taken place—oh, how final and sad it felt.
Grim. The curtains were drawn back as if she were still
in there, Mrs B. keeping the show on the road. But who
would do the garden, and what would happen to everything now? To whom had childless Jenny left it all? Pre-
sumably the niece, but would she want it? And if not,
who would come to live there?

Persephone put her foot down and drove away, meeting in half a mile the blank-faced Stop/Go boy, at it again, this time with the council hedge-trimmer, slowly roaring its way along the road and leaving devastation. It ripped, it tore, it left the towering hawthorn with ragged branches stripped of their bark and dangling, the ditches with their clouds of cow parsley and ragged robin all cut through, heaped up to die in the sun. She sat and waited, as holiday traffic drove past, coming out of the town to visit all the pretty villages. At least it was sunny: might that help Henry, on his long sad drive?

The sign swung round to Go. She went.

The town was crowded, but she found a space in the car park and set forth with her basket: to the butcher for a leg of lamb, which she would roast very slowly with garlic and rosemary—summer or no, there was nothing like the smell of a roast to lift the spirits as you arrived, and it would last her all week. Then to the deli. The town, once an ordinary working place, had in the last few years had a serious makeover: a deli where there used to be a caff, an interiors shop full of pale blankets, distressed tables, dried lavender in enamel jugs. Charity shops looked like boutiques, and boutiques (where Jenny had shopped) like something out of Marylebone High Street.

All very pretty, and prosperous beneath those sheep-strewn hills, yet faintly unreal and, in these tough times, perhaps unlikely to last. Never mind: today she could not think about local recession and unemployment and what—perhaps—she might do to help. She must get on. And she bought the pâté and olives and a nice nutty loaf from the deli and came out feeling some sense of accomplishment. Now, then.

—Hello, Persephone!

She jumped, found herself gazing at someone she had met before, but could not place.

—I'm Elizabeth, said the smiling woman before her, as she had said, hand extended, at the funeral. — I'm so sorry: did I startle you?

—Not at all, said Persephone, at once resistant, as she had been in that crowded village hall. She had not wanted to be greeted with such familiar warmth by a total stranger, and she did not want now to be put at a disadvantage. A mother with a pushchair and another child in tow came up behind her and she moved to get out of the way on the narrow pavement, thus able to avoid that New Age smile. That's what it was: something from a parallel universe of encounter groups and singing, and getting to know one another: some touchy-feely ghastliness which Jenny had somehow been involved with. How on earth?

—Nice to see you, she said coolly, as she had said down the years at countless drinks parties, making her getaway from the dull, the hopeful. — You're ruthless, David Cheetham had said to her once, and it was true. — I'm afraid I'm in a bit of a hurry, she said now, but Elizabeth put a hand on her arm.

—Have you got time for a coffee? Just a quick one? I so wanted to talk to you yesterday.

—Why was that? asked Persephone, in a tone just this side of outright rudeness.

—Jenny talked about you: I recognised you straight away. She said how distinctive you were. I don't want to intrude, but the day after a funeral is always so dreadful, isn't it? I'm going back to London this afternoon, I'd so appreciate—

Persephone gave up. She took her—she would not let herself be taken—to The Old Wheel, three doors down, led the way to the only table left, ordered the coffee.

—You were going to tell me, she said, as the waitress left them,—about Music for Life. Is that what it's called? Where you met Jenny.

—That's right. She was such a gifted person, wasn't she? That lovely voice. And the piano—we all play what's there, or take our instruments. I take my violin. Or we just sing. And of course we talk a lot, between workshops: that's what we all need.

Had Jenny needed to talk? wondered Persephone, as the coffee arrived. Hadn't she had more friends than anyone? Not to mention Henry—

—Jenny never told you about us?

—She didn't, no.

—We're all cancer patients, said Elizabeth, with that warm bright smile. —That's what brings us together. We're all musical, but Music for Life gives us a space to talk about—well, what we're going through.

—I see, said Persephone slowly, and then could say no more. Around them the crowded room was full of talk and chatter, but she felt herself in a pool of silence.

—I've surprised you, said Elizabeth. —I'm so sorry. Jenny said you were very reserved.

—I—did she?

—But she was terribly fond of you. Terribly. And you sounded so interesting——all your background, and everything. I had a good career myself, in public relations, but nothing like yours. Whitehall! Right at the heart of everything. Anyway—she lifted her cup to her lips. —Then I got ill.

Persephone heard herself murmur that she was sorry, but from a great, peculiar distance. She sipped her coffee, and felt her heart begin to race. But it wasn't the caffeine, it was something like shock. That Jenny should have chosen to talk, not to her, but to strangers. She heard that fluting voice, responding to enquiries—Oh, I'm all right, you know. Coping. How are you? She said that to everyone, when all the time—Not even Henry had known where she went.

—Where do you meet? she asked Elizabeth.

—Not so far from here. Do you know Great Brobury?

Persephone nodded. A village with a duck pond, somewhere tourists loved, though she hadn't been there for years.

—Just outside, said Elizabeth.—A converted barn, you've probably passed it.

She probably had. And there Jenny had gone, and talked about what she was going through, and talked about her friends—about her, Persephone, to whom she had said nothing.

—It's a beautiful place, lovely gardens, all owned by the Trust. I don't know what I'd do without it. We all come away feeling so much better—it's like a retreat, I suppose, except we all talk so much! Mind you, you can be quiet if you want to, of course. People go off by themselves, that's fine. Jenny did, quite often.

—Did she?

That Persephone, now, should be asking someone she did not know about the woman she had liked almost better than anyone—it was intolerable. Had Jenny lived, had Henry been bolder, or less kind, she might have been her sister-in-law. Of course Henry had wanted to marry her, of course he had—

She heard herself asking if Jenny had talked about many of her friends, took a deep breath and asked if she had talked about men.

—Men? said Elizabeth.—I don't think so, no. Of course she was so attractive, wasn't she, I'm sure lots of men were keen on her, but she never mentioned anyone, only talked about you, and a few other village people. Why? Was there anyone special?

—No, said Persephone.

And as she finished her coffee she was left to contemplate her own banging down of the shutters with that lie, and the ways in which Jenny had lived so privately: telling no one about her weekends away, telling no one, when she stayed in that music-filled barn, about the man she had adored—secretly from all except Persephone—and made so happy. Who was now quite broken.

—I must go, she said abruptly, and then, partly to deflect attention from the man in Jenny's life, for surely Elizabeth knew that she had lied, and partly out of awful curiosity, she said:—Forgive me, I don't mean to pry, but you said you were ill. And the people who were with you yesterday, Johann and—

—Maggie. Self-effacing Maggie.

—Yes. They also—

—Have cancer? Yes. We're all in remission, of course. But Johann—perhaps he doesn't have very long.

—He's so young.

—Twenty-three.

—Dear God.

And Persephone was silent.

—It's everywhere, said Elizabeth.—Don't you find that?

—Not exactly.

Persephone cast her mind back down all the long years of her life, remembering colleagues and friends who had slipped away, out of the swim and into the remote reaches of illness, where she, who was never ill, had rarely followed. Flowers to hospital, yes, sometimes a visit, a funeral attended, but, until Jenny, never that day-by-day enquiry, that doing things, that being there, that care. Even her parents —

— I must go, she said again, and pushed back her chair. — I — what could she say? — I do hope you do well.

— Thank you, said Elizabeth. — It was such a pleasure to meet you.

And why was that? thought Persephone, but managed not to say it, and rose from her seat, just as Elizabeth told her that Jenny had left her cottage to Music for Life.

The lamb was in the oven, and the fire was lit: even in June it could be chilly, and it was. Persephone, watching for Henry's car, observed the sky above the Green clouding over again. One or two cars came and went, but not his, not yet.

— Oh, come on, Henry.

She found she was longing — yes, longing — for his arrival. The table was laid, more roses at its centre: everything looked welcoming and bright. She thought: if he had not been coming, I should not have gone into town; I should not have been so shaken; should not have felt this need to confide, nor so hoped for his company. And yet — what would he make of Jenny's secret life? And was it making too much of it all, to think of it like that? Didn't everyone withhold things, especially in crisis, even from their closest friends and family?

She realised that she did not know. She didn't know what people did in intimate relationships. And when Henry had come down here, as often as he thought he could, which wasn't often; when he parked his car outside her cottage, walking with her up to Jenny's so that neighbours would think the two of them were going, quite innocently, for a pleasant supper; when she, later, had walked briskly home alone, she had never allowed herself to think of what followed her departure. Bad enough to be colluding in deception, let alone dwelling on what it involved. She came home, turned on the television or picked up her book, turned her mind away.

—How strange, she said aloud, and realised that she was thinking of her own life.—Oh, come on, Henry, she said again, impatiently, suddenly unable to be alone a moment longer.

And there he was, coming slowly along the road, slowing still more at Jenny's house, then picking up speed until he pulled up behind her own car at the gate. He did not get out straight away, and she did not like to intrude upon this moment of arrival, this return. So she turned from the window, and waited for his knock, putting another log on the fire, looking in the mirror to straighten her hair, as if—Good heavens, she thought suddenly—as if she were waiting for a lover. How absurd.

Then she heard his footsteps coming slowly up the path, and went to the door to greet him.

—Henry.

He had aged, he had aged, all the life gone out of him.

—Come in, let me get you a drink.

He nodded, came in with his overnight bag.

—Your room is all ready.

—Thanks. I'll just go up and—

—See you in a minute. When you're ready.

And as he climbed the stairs she went to the drinks cupboard, to the fridge for ice, and the olives, and prepared the mahogany tray, which had once belonged to her parents, who, in those long-distant summers, had farmed her out with Henry, and had him to stay in return.

—Henry?

She heard her voice sounding all down the years, calling him in house and garden, where they had mooched about together, played cricket for two, done jigsaws on rainy afternoons. One—she had it somewhere still—showed a Victorian village scene, with hollyhocks and a little girl with a hoop, bowling away down the lane, which stretched into hazy distance. How sad it made her, all at once, to think of all that now.

—Henry?

—Coming.

Here he was. He gave what he could of a smile, he took the glass she gave him.

—Thanks. Thanks so much. Well, now—

They sat on either side of the fire. She could hear him making the most enormous effort, as perhaps he had done all his life, until Jenny.

—Well, now, Persephone. How have you been?

—Oh, Henry—

And then—but how was this happening, when she was supposed to be comforting him? Why did she feel so, so—what did she feel? Everything, everything, a great loosening inside her, as if an ice floe had come adrift and was floating away, unstoppably, beneath the darkest sky. And then he was beside her, putting his glass down, murmuring—I know, I know, and holding her hand as she wept.

Last Fling

Last Fling. Musical F, 60, ill and unlikely to recover, seeks tall, kind, clever man for loving companionship in whatever time is left.

— ARE YOU MAD? said Steff.
The phone rang off the hook. This, however, was in response, not to the ad (you picked up your messages on voicemail), but to the card Steff had put in the post office window, looking for a cleaner, four hours a week, family home, some ironing, reliable, refs please, car if poss.

— I can't go to work, look after you and do the cleaning.

— I don't see why not.

From the relative comfort of her post-op bed — books, hot water bottle, cat — most things seemed possible to Fran, as long as she herself was not required to do them. The phone rang again. Steff paced up and down, asking questions; Fran, at a nod, wrote down the name and contact number.

— What else could a number be for, except contact?

— People roam about: I suppose it means mobile. Steff replaced the phone in its cradle by the bed and stood looking out of the window.

— We don't want a roaming cleaner, said Fran, watching her. Steff looked tired round the edges: already the strain was beginning to tell, and things had hardly started yet.

— I' m not going to ask how long I have left, Fran had told her consultant, in the privacy of his cubbyhole at the city's crumbling hospital. — No one can ever tell, can they? Not really.

— Not really, no.

— I just want to live as good a life as I can. Until I can't.

— How wise. He reached for her file and explained her treatment. It sounded vile: he assured her that most people tolerated it well. Then he took off his specs and smiled at her with genuine encouragement: a tall, kind, clever and attractive man some fifteen years younger than she, and Fran put her hand to her hair, to the scalloped jet clasp which had once belonged to her mother, and which now held up the well-cut fall of grey.

— What did he say? asked Steff, as they drove away. The crumbling hospital was being rebuilt: chaps in hard hats strode about beneath clouds and cranes and scaffolding, shouting happily.

— I'll tell you when we get home.

— Okay, said Steff later, pen and paper in hand. — I've whittled it down to five. She shifted on the edge of the bed, and Fran bit back a wince. — Interviews on Friday, half an hour each, with gaps for getaways. How does that sound?

— Exhausting, said Fran, stroking Perseus. — Whittle it down a bit more.

— You don't have to see them all.

— Yes, I do.

— Don't you trust me?

— No.

—How about a little nap before lunch?

—Good idea.

When she woke up, the hot water bottle was cold and Dorcas had left her. Fran lay watching the wintry clouds and bare trees across the field, then sat up a little. Now she could see the muddy lane which ran between their box hedge and the farmer's field, empty and full of rusty clumps of sorrel. Grim.

—Grim, she said aloud, and reached for the phone.

—What's that? asked Steff, coming up the stairs with the lunch tray.

—The field. Fran put down the phone.—It needs sheep and lambs.

—They'll be here soon enough, then we won't get a wink of sleep. Who were you phoning?

—Never mind.

—Checking for replies? Steff put the tray on Fran's lap and a comforting cloud of steam rose from two bowls of homemade minestrone. Warm rolls were wrapped in a napkin, the butter was fresh.

—You're completely wonderful.

—You'd do it for me.

—Don't count on it. Fran unwrapped her roll.—How are the interviews?

—I've got it down to three. We start at ten. Steff settled herself in the button-backed chair, with Fran's soup and plate on the bedside table, pushed up against books, phone, little vase of snowdrops, tablets, empty glass.—Shall I fill that for you? For the lunchtime tabs?

—That would be kind.

They had their lunch companionably, discussing the possible merits of Carole, (no car but experience as a carer), Tonya, single parent of a little one at nursery (sounded keen) and Cheryl, single parent of three, made redundant (sounded desperate).

— All these redundancies.

— All these single parents.

Stephanie and Frances, single childless sisters, finished their soup and rolls. Fran had no strength for an apple. A wintry gleam of afternoon sun lit up the room, showing all the get-well cards and dust.

— Look at that. We do need a cleaner. Please God you won't be made redundant.

— Indeed. And I'd better get back there. Now then: anything you need? Steff lifted the tray and brushed away crumbs.

— I don't think so. Send up Perseus if you see him.

— He can bring a fresh hot water bottle.

When all this had been accomplished, and when she could hear Steff backing the car out, setting forth along the lane to the main road, and thence the garden centre, Fran reached once more for the phone. Not a single message. Not one. Only an automated voice announcing this, though the added— 'today' offered (perhaps) a glimmer of hope for tomorrow.

— (A) Who would take you on? Steff had asked last week. (B) What kind of person would they be if they did? (C) You're putting yourself At Risk. Seriously.

— Oh, do shut up. I wish I'd never told you.

Steff passed the chocolate biscuits. Fran took one, then couldn't face it.

— Have you never felt a flicker of hope or longing? she asked. — I don't mean when we were young. I mean latterly. As the years go by.

— I gave up hope long ago, said Steff contentedly, unwrapping gold foil.

—Well, said Fran, watching the sun sink low behind the trees,—I want to have one last go. I'd like to meet someone nice who could take me out to dinner, or a concert, or just go for a walk along the coast—

—It's freezing on the coast. And you're in bed half the time: where would you find the energy for all that?

—Perhaps it would give me the energy. You should be encouraging me. You should say I've got spirit.

—You have, said Steff.—Go on, then. Give it a go.

Perseus slumbered at her feet; the house was quiet. Next week the chemo began. In the last pleasant interlude before all that took over, Fran lay back against the pillows, watching the February sky begin to darken. Gulls blown inland headed out again; rooks made for the trees across the field. She had lived here almost all her life: something so few people could say now, and few expected.

You expected to leave, to work, to marry, to make your own home.

Perseus shifted, as Fran moved her feet, growing sleepy with thinking about the past: its fullness and enormous emptiness. Life in London. Life in London! The Guildhall, the Royal College; forming the quartet. The concerts in churches, at local festivals and in grand private houses, waiting for the Wigmore Hall to take notice, getting the Purcell Room at last. Bravo! They hadn't done so badly. On Saturday mornings her family might hear news of their Schubert recording on CD Review; they might see an ad in the Sunday paper: in the listings for the Barbican, or St John's Smith Square. Schubert and Haydn and Brahms. Beethoven late. Her parents came down to hear them, taking Fran's bedroom for the night while she, lovesick, tried to sleep on the sofa.

❧

Daniel Solomon was slender and tall, with a flop of dark hair and a nervous energy which made him both creative and liable to drop things. He dropped a knife and fork with a clatter the first time he and Fran had lunch, in the Royal College canteen, and banged his head on the table as he rose from picking them up. He apologised with an unnervingly sweet smile.

Daniel was often apologetic, but commanding in performance, and ambitious.

That he should have asked Fran to join the quartet, with himself on first violin, she on second, Abigail Joyce on viola and Christopher Bell on cello, was the most flattering and exciting thing that had ever happened to her. For years, the music, their work, and Daniel, were the centre of her life.

Meanwhile, Steff, the green-fingered one, stayed in Suffolk, trained as a landscape gardener, and joined what was effectively another quartet: two men and two women, out in all weathers and strong. Landscape gardening wasn't just about design — those great big sheets of paper spread over the kitchen table, the flower beds, the climbers, the pergola and herringbone path. It was huge sacks of compost, great slabs of York stone or crazy paving, piles of brick, the cement mixer sloshing away. The van took the four of them, two in the front and two in the back, squashed up against spades and forks and pruners. What a laugh.

Life in London, on a quarter-share of a concert, a quarter-share of a recording contract, a few private lessons here and there, began to be unaffordable. And much too painful. Abigail and Christopher, fitting into one another's lives and background like instruments in their handmade leather cases, were married within two years. Daniel and Fran did not achieve this. After months of trying to ignore his nervous but determined withdrawal, Fran confronted him. They went for a terrible walk along the Embankment, in the rain. Leaves swirled down from the plane trees, tugboats rocked on the tide.

—I love you, she said hopelessly. —I shall always love you.

Daniel eventually, nervously and tenderly, told her he had met someone else. The tenderness undid her.

—This could break the quartet, she said bleakly, when she could cry no more, and knew as she spoke that it was already breaking, and that she, by leaving, would make that final.

—Better to have loved and lost than never to have loved at all, said her mother, folding her in her arms.

—Have this, said her father, pouring a double.

—Never get involved with people at work, said Steff, taking her boots off. —It's the number one rule.

—It didn't feel like work. It felt like home.

—Fatal.

Fran climbed upstairs with her violin, to weep in the room of her childhood. She was twenty-nine.

In the end—I'll never play again / Don't be ridiculous / Never / You can always teach / I don't want to *teach*!—in the end, she found another life. She retrained, in concert management, and became someone quite different. The tired old hall on the coast where, as a child, she had heard Tortellier and du Pre, was being renovated with lavish EU funding. She got a job there, as programme assistant;

she went on a course. By the time the arts had become the creative industries, she had become an efficient and successful fundraiser. By the time you could not plan a season without planning a creative partnership, she was in dialogue with every local school and college, attracting sponsorship from national business.

Sometimes, she looked back on her old life, and at her life now, with wonder: that an artist could, over time, become an administrator, no matter how creative, made her think that perhaps she had not, after all, been a true artist, and that this was why Daniel had abandoned her.

By this time, their father had been dead for fifteen years, buried in the church of their childhood on a bright March day, leaving the three of them to grieve and regroup into a female family of three. A coven, said their mother, bright and brave. Fran and Steff did not use this word. Their mother walked the dog (male) and played bridge. She did the flowers in the church, where Fran, from time to time, played again, in another quartet where the others were married, or gay. They did weddings, and birthday parties in houses whose gardens had been done by Steff. Fran no longer allowed herself to think of Daniel. After a long time, she began to imagine that someone else—surely, someone else—might replace him.

No one did. Somehow it just didn't happen. Was it because heartbreak had taken its toll, and it showed? Was there something about her, now, that simply didn't belong? Nothing happened to Steff, either, with her cropped hair and jeans and muddy boots, though none of these things indicated anything other than dedication to work and simple preference. She'd always been a tomboy.

—But not—

—Not for a moment.

As the years passed, they stopped talking about men

altogether. By the time their mother died—buried beside their father on an afternoon in June—she, too, had long since given up her hopeful enquiries: Nice evening? Anyone interesting there? Was Robert there?

No one was there, and that was an end of it.

And now the room of my childhood has become a sick-room, thought Fran, turning over as the sky grew dark. She switched on the bedside light, lay looking for a while at the cards propped up on the chest of drawers: from the village, from the tame quartet, from work. *Hope to see you as soon as you're up to a visit.* And *Sweetheart! Get well soon! All our love, Vivian and the Box Office.* All that life, which felt so distant now. She must not sink: she must try to look good. She felt for her bag—everything, these days, lay within reach on the bed—and her mirror. What a fright. Already. Weight loss and pallor and more grey hair. Steff's clear voice rang in her ears: Who would take you on? What kind of person would they be?

Someone brave and kind, thought Fran, brushing her hair—was she going to lose it? She'd have to give up if she lost it. Someone who doesn't want a long involvement himself—why? Perhaps he's ill himself, perhaps we can comfort one another, have tea by the fire, walk down the lane as the weather grows warmer. Blossom will blow from the orchard. The word helpmeet, sweet and old-fashioned, and unheard of nowadays, came into her mind as she gazed into the mirror. Dark eyes looked back at her. Thin and pale as she was, her flesh was still firm and her lips, parted in an enquiring smile, revealed still-pretty teeth. I was good-looking, she thought, putting the mirror and brush back. Daniel told me I was beautiful, over and over again. One might perhaps have expected that Steff might miss the boat, but surely I should have—

What a traitorous thought. How unsisterly and how unkind.

True, however, and not the first time she had thought it.

She reached for the phone: you never knew.

Yes, you did.

Perseus stretched to his fullest extent, his paws quivering with the effort.

—As for you, said Fran.

On Saturday she got up after breakfast and reported for duty.

—Dressed and in my right mind, she told Steff, who was loading the dishwasher.

A car pulled up in the lane and they looked at the clock.

—She's early.

—Remind me which—

—Carole.

—Redundant?

—That was Cheryl. This is the carer.

—Very good. Let us gird up our loins for the fray.

—If you talk to them like that, said Steff, going to the front door, —We won't get anyone. —I'll introduce you, then show her the house, then bring her back again. Okay?

—Sure, said Fran to the empty kitchen. Weak sunshine lit up the windowsill, the hyacinths, coming up nicely. It was some time since she'd been down here except in her dressing gown, and she felt suddenly so well that she that she thought: I could go back to work. Easy. I could say I didn't want the chemo, go back to my independent life and—

—This is Carole, said Steff, striding in. —My sister Fran.

—Pleased to meet you, said Carole. She was small and plump, with wispy hair and pale watery eyes. A sad little thing, it seemed.

—How do you do? said Fran, rising.

—Not too bad. Isn't it cold?

—Do you want to keep your coat on? asked Steff. —While I show you round?

—I think I will, if you don't mind.

—I don't mind at all. Right, then.

And so the morning passed. Fran made them coffee, and told each of them, since Steff had said she must, that she wasn't well, and might be in bed some of the time. Steff questioned each one closely, Fran asked if they themselves had questions, and made light of her condition. Perseus was introduced.

—How old is he?

—Ten. He's the one in charge here, we just do what he tells us.

—Nice to have a man about the place, said Tonya. —I could do with that myself. Mind if I smoke?

—Yes, said Steff and Fran together.

In the end, over lunch, they settled on Cheryl. She appeared capable and resilient—had weathered divorce and redundancy, was bringing up the kids—and though she had sounded desperate on the phone, once here had seemed cheerful and kind.

—I'll ring her references, said Steff, making coffee. —Peppermint tea for you?

—Please. And I'll take it back to bed.

How had she thought she was fit to return to work? A morning up, three interviews, and she was on her knees, had almost asked Steff if she could have lunch on a tray, but made herself stay up: if she didn't make an effort, where would it end?

You know where it's going to end, she told herself, sinking back on to the pillows. Oh, that was better.

—What's going to end? asked Steff, coming in with a jug of catkins.

—Was I talking aloud?

—You were. Steff set the jug on the chest of drawers and turned to look at her. —How are you feeling?

—Terrific, said Fran, observing the complete uplifting beauty of that jug. —Thank you, Steff. I think I'll go to sleep now. Any joy with the refs?

—One was out. I'm going to work in the garden. See you at teatime.

—Very good. Fran reached for the radio—to hell with the phone—and fell asleep listening to the afternoon play, so poor that it sent her off almost at once. When she awoke, the sky was darkening once more and there was a programme about landfill sites. She retuned to *Afternoon on Three* and found—oh, oh heavens—

How many times had she played in this?

It was not unusual to have this experience, of course: over the years, any number of radio choices or concerts might include something from their repertoire. Less usual to have one of their own recordings—yet here it was, she knew it at once, the *Brahms A Minor Quartet 52 Opus*, the most demanding work they had ever played, recorded for EMI over three exhausting days.

Fran, filled with emotion, lay listening to them all, she on second violin and Daniel on the first, seeing again, as clearly as if he were in the room, the flop of hair, the hands which Durer might have drawn; hearing the intake of breath at the start of the second movement which—with

many difficult passages — they had had to edit out, and
re-record.

— I loved you, she said aloud, and began to cry. — I
really did love you. And with these words her youth
came flooding back, with all its hope and passion, two
things now so utterly absent from her life, except for what
seemed all at once such a cheap, shallow idea. To adver-
tise for some stranger! To put her condition in a national
newspaper!

— Darling, said Steff, coming in with the tea
tray. — Darling, whatever's wrong?

— Nothing, sobbed Fran, as the last notes died away
and Petroc Trelawney told them they'd been listening to
the Solomon Quartet.

Chemotherapy began on Monday. So did Cheryl, whose
references made it clear they could safely leave her, once
she'd been shown the ropes. Two mornings a week,
petrol paid, £8.50 an hour, at least to start with. She
waved them off as they drove away and it felt as if she had
always been there. The morning was windy and bright.
Lambs were in every field except theirs.

— Bet you any money they'll be there when we get
back, said Steff.

Fran took her arm as they walked across the hospital car
park; it was bitingly cold. Steff stayed with her as they put
the line in through a vein in her arm, to a place unnervingly close to her heart. The procedure was entirely pain-
less and the nurse, discovering Fran's interests, revealed
that she herself wrote folk songs.

— You must come to one of my gigs.

Then they went through to the ward, where five or
six people were already hooked up to intravenous drips,
sitting in huge plastic armchairs. Some were alone, others

had someone with them, one or two were eating sand-wiches. A young man in blue tunic and trousers came over.

—Are you Frances Page? Hi, my name's Pete, I'm your nurse for the day.

—How nice, said Fran, and it was.

The hours she had been dreading passed in a perfectly acceptable manner: intravenous anti-sickness drug, the start of the chemo drug itself, the friendly words with the woman in the next chair, the sandwiches which Steff had made just in case she really wanted them, which she did. After this, she had a little nap, while Steff read the paper. When she woke up, there was a note beside her: BACK SOON.

Fran looked up at her drip: about two-thirds done. She sat watching everyone: the quiet, still patients, the translucent bags of drugs hanging above them; the busy nurses in their blue and white uniforms; the sudden shaft of sunlight through the window, touching all of them with pale butter-yellow. Cancer Ward. A painting, if she could only paint.

Steff came back with a pretty little tote bag.

—What's that?

—Something for a brave girl.

Fran smiled, looked inside to find a cellophane-wrapped box of scent.

—Madame Rochas! What joy. Thank you, Steff.

Soon it was time to go home. A bottle in a canvas bag was hooked around her waist, pumping in another drug. A district nurse would come and take it off on Wednes-day. She had pills to take.

—It's all go, said Steff.

—You'll be fine, said Pete, patting Fran's arm. —Just take it easy for a few days.

—I've forgotten how to take it any other way.

As they turned off the main road and into their lane, the calls of lambs were everywhere.

—What did I tell you? asked Steff.

The field across from the house was alive with shaggy ewes and their lambs, skipping, butting, crying in the wind.

—Oh, how wonderful.

—Earplugs, said Steff. —I wonder how Cheryl got on.

As soon as they opened the front door they could feel the difference. The smell of furniture polish, the vacuumed rugs, swept stairs and sparkling kitchen: everything felt calm and well-kept. She'd left a note: HOPE IT WASN'T TOO BAD. SEE YOU WEDNESDAY.

—We did a good thing there, said Steff. —What would you like for supper?

There are periods in life which are especially vivid; then the weeks swim by. For Fran, that week before her treatment began remained etched in her mind: the appearance of her advertisement, with all its attendant hope and disappointment; the dark afternoons when she lay in bed, warm and comfortable but with death never far from her thoughts; the sudden rush of pain and regret as the memory of love returned.

After that, she settled into her new routine of chemo, blood tests and check-ups. Had she said she wanted to live a good life? There seemed no room for much life at all; they seemed to be driving in to hospital almost as soon as they came back. She had an emergency number to call if she felt ill, but she didn't: tired, yes, but her bed was her closest friend. She had a sore mouth, but that her consultant sorted out quite early, lowering her dose.

—Does that mean it'll be less effective? That I won't last as long?

—It'll still be effective. How do you feel you're coping?

—Okay so far.

—Well done. Again he gave her a smile of real warmth and kindness, and she thought, returning it: You're just the kind of man I like; you're exactly the kind of man I had in mind when I placed that silly ad, only you're too young. And married, of course, like all consultants. It was true: she'd never seen one yet without a wedding ring, it must go with the job.

He coughed. —Right, then, I'll see you in a couple of weeks. Look after yourself.

And she went out, blushing, into the crowded clinic. How could all these people have cancer? Most of them looked perfectly well, though here and there a ghost leaned against friend or partner, with clothes hanging off them, thin hair, candle-coloured skin.

Steff was waiting, doing the crossword. This afternoon, she'd be back at work.

—He's lowered the dose, Fran told her, as they drove home. Spring was here at last, everything soft and fresh.

—Has he now? said Steff, and Fran could feel her unspoken thought.

—It's no less effective. That's what he said.

—I'm glad to hear it.

And they returned to the house, with the lambs racing about in the field and the smell of ironed laundry greeting them as soon as they opened the door.

—Hi there, called Cheryl from the kitchen. —Get on all right?

As the weeks wore on, things began to change. Tiredness became a deep fatigue, such as she had never known. Where she had begun to come down for meals, with only the occasional supper on a tray, now she could hardly sit at the table, hardly lift their parents' silver—a wedding present—to raise a mouthful to her lips. Food tasted different, her tongue full of a strange metallic taste. She pushed the plate away, put her head on her arms.

—Come on, old thing.

—I can't. Sorry.

—Just another mouthful? For Perseus?

She managed a smile.—Sorry. I'm going back to bed.

But then she had to climb those stairs, looming like Everest before her.

—You're like an old donkey, said Steff, giving her an arm.

—Thanks.

In bed at last, she closed her eyes, felt swimmy, opened them again, caught Steff's unguarded expression, anxiety etched into every line.

—I'm so sorry, she said: it seemed she was always saying it.—This isn't much fun for you.

—Don't be ridiculous. It's you who's going through all this.

—Yes, but—

But she was too weary to speak.

—Two more doses, said Steff, sitting in the button-backed chair which had once been in their parents' bedroom.—Just two more and then it's over. We'll go on an outing, as soon as you feel well again. We could have a little holiday—would you like that?

—Perhaps.

Next time they went to the clinic they gave her a blood transfusion.

—That'll perk you up.

It did. She stopped planning her funeral, and the relentless question, which she still refused to ask—How long? How long?—began to fade.

It was over, it was done, she was still here. A couple of weeks after the last dose—Well done, you've done brilliantly, see you in three months, go and do something nice now—they did something nice.

On the anniversary of their mother's death, a beautiful morning in June, they drove to the coast. It was a journey Fran had made almost every day of her working life, in all weathers, often returning late at night after a concert, seeing a fox slink into the hedgerow as she came down their lane, an owl rise suddenly from a gate post, sweeping low across the fields.

She had gone to work? For all those years? She had run things, planned things, talked to people, rushed about?

That was in another country, and besides, the wench is dead.

A long-forgotten line from A-level Shakespeare, and the school play, came floating down the decades: *The Merchant of Venice*, she in the school orchestra playing in the interval; Mr Fisher, the head of music, getting them involved with every blessed thing.

She had played in an orchestra? Gone to the Royal College, been part of a well-known quartet?

Fallen in love?

—What a deep sigh, said Steff, as the concert hall buildings came into view and they had their first glimpse of the sea.—A penny for your thoughts.

—Just—What could she say?—Just the past. Sorry. It all seems so impossible now. That I ever did any of it.

—You did it all. You did it very well. Now let's concentrate on today.

They pulled into the car park, pulled on their

jackets—even in June, the sea breeze could cut right through you—and walked, arm in arm, along the prom.

—I feel like an old lady.

The sea was a broken blue-green, the waves crashed on to the pebbles and sucked them out again, clouds raced over the sun. Far out, a fishing boat rose and fell, and the gulls were shrieking.

—Bracing, I think you'd call it, even in June, Do you feel braced?

—Sort of.

—Too cold?

—It's okay. Stop worrying.

They descended the little flight of concrete steps and walked on the beach, crunch crunch. It was Friday—Steff had taken the day off—and those on the beach were mothers and pre-school children, or people walking the dog: retired couples or single people, calling as a Labrador or mixed-breed mutt pelted joyously into the water.

As she watched all this activity, Fran felt something like happiness come stealing into her: she drew a deep breath, and leaned on Steff's shoulder.

—Thanks for bringing me.

They had lunch in the concert hall restaurant, sitting in a window seat warmed by the sun. In the old days Fran would have been in here with a sponsor, a journalist or conductor, dressed up, buying lunch on expenses. Or she'd have been at her desk with a sandwich, catching up with email. Now here she was, a new member of the retired-through-ill-health club, and as she looked round the restaurant she wondered: How many people in here have had cancer? It's everywhere, it's like a plague, that heaving clinic is just one part of it. There are plenty of people like me out and about who've been through it all, who are living like me through the last of their days, trying to make the most of it.

—I think I'll have the warmed goat's cheese as a starter, said Steff.—What about you? Fran? You've gone into a dream again.

—Sorry.

—Have something hot as a main course: you need to warm up, I can tell.

It was true: a shank of local lamb, glazed with orange and honey, brought back that fleeting sense of happiness and wellbeing, even if she couldn't eat it all. The ticking question—how long? how long?—had almost gone. Perhaps she could beat it, after all. Look at Roger Norrington—given six months to live years and years ago, and as busy and alive as ever. This time last year he'd been up here with the Orchestra of the Age of Enlightenment and—

—Fran? Fran!

A voice rang out across the restaurant, and there was Vivian Welch, he of the Box Office, waving and weaving his way through the tables towards them.

—My dear—I didn't recognise you. How *are* you? You must have been through the *mill*.

—How lovely to see you, said Fran.—Do I look ghastly?

—No, darling, no of course not, I just mean it's been such a long time, we've all been thinking of you so much, you should have told us you were coming.

—Well, you know what it's like. Do sit down—you remember my sister Stephanie?

—Of course! How are *you*? Vivian pulled out a chair.

—Very well, thanks. Glass of wine?

—What I mean is, said Fran, as they got going—You know what it's like when people come back to work after they've left. Lethal. They want to talk and talk and you just want to get on. I didn't want to be a spectre at the feast, sort of thing.

—Honestly, said Vivian, putting down his glass.—Only you could say that, Fran, when we've all been so worried about you. You must come up and say hello to everyone, they'll be thrilled.

—We'll see. I'm sure they're all up to their eyes.

Vivian turned to Steff.—What's happened to the girl?

—I know, said Steff.—She apologises every time she opens her mouth—she's so self-effacing she's almost disappeared.

—Oh, don't say that, said Vivian, raising his glass again.—Cheers! To health and happiness!

In the end, they didn't go up to the offices.—Another time, said Fran, feeling exhaustion hit her once again.—Sorry. Give them all my love.

—I will, said Vivian.—And you take the greatest care.

The afternoon sun had warmed the car; Fran sank back in her seat and fell asleep almost at once, waking as Steff pulled up outside the house. Swallows were darting along the sunlit lane.

—Sorry, she said, yawning.—Have I really slept the whole way?

As Mother would say, you must have needed it. Steff pulled out the key.—I was thinking: I might just walk up to the churchyard, take her some roses. What do you think?

—We should have done it this morning. I'll come with you.

—Are you sure? Aren't you worn out?

—No. Fran stretched, and opened her door, getting stiffly out.—I must build up my strength.

So they walked down the lane with an armful of roses from the garden and the swallows skimmed before them. And Fran thought, with sudden clarity: by the time they're gathering on the wire, I'll be gone.

But the smell of summer grass! As they walked quietly along the path from the lych gate, they breathed it in, and she said to herself: This is one of the things I shall miss, an absurd thought which felt quite reasonable. They came to their parents' graves, on the far side beneath a line of yew. Sun filtered through, but it was colder here, and she shivered, taking the roses as Steff bent down to pick up the sunken vase and carried it across to the standing tap. The sound of running water filled the air, the scent of the roses in Fran's arms was rich and heady. Birds called from every tree, and a wagtail, her father's favourite bird, ran suddenly across the grass before her. In this intense and perfect moment, Steff's returning footsteps sounding on the path, she turned, still shivering a little, towards the shaded headstones where her parents' names were carved, lichen creeping towards them.

— See you soon, she said quietly, although she, like her sister, had long since abandoned faith: childhood's bright and beautiful, cast away.

Then Steff was beside her, setting the vase back in place, and they both knelt down on the cool grass to fill it with the long-stemmed roses, pink and cream and yellow, and got up again — how stiff she was, how really cold now — and stood in silence, two daughters who in late middle-age had found themselves — so unexpectedly, at first by default, and then through feeling — each other's true companion.

— You're cold, said Steff.

— I am a bit.

— Let's go.

As they walked slowly home, Fran said suddenly—I'm not going to have a last fling.

—So I gathered.

—I cancelled the ad. Ages ago. It was a silly idea.

—It was brave.

—That's not what you said at the time.

—No. Well. I just didn't want to see you get hurt.

—Thanks. Anyway—it all seems a long time ago, the whole thing. All that treatment—

—It's wiped it all away?

—Sort of. Pretty much.

Shadows were lengthening, a cloud of midges danced in the last of the sun, sheep without their lambs cropped the grass unendingly. As they came through their gate Perseus came round the house to greet them.

—How about a whisky? Now you can drink again.

—What a very good idea.

She fell asleep thinking of Daniel. Someone must tell him: he would want to know. She woke in the middle of the night, shaking from head to foot. I've caught my death, she thought, right in the middle of summer. Feverish wordplay filled her. Could you catch your death? Wasn't it death who caught you? Beyond her curtained window she could hear an owl—a little owl, with that high-pitched cry, a creature she had known all her life, just part of the night, and being here, but now it sounded frightening and shrill, and she reached, trembling, to switch on the lamp. The pool of light on radio and glass and pile of books brought instant relief: she was safe, the shadowy room around her full of things she cared about: that chair, with the rug folded over the back, those old watercolours, the jug on the chest which Steff had filled with roses, her violin, resting in the corner. She would never play again.

She closed her eyes and her head pounded, and still she shivered and shook.

— Steff? Steff?

At last she came, barefoot, tugging on her dressing gown, hair sticking up like a scarecrow.

— What? What is it?

— I think I've caught something, I'm so sorry.

— Let's have a look at you. Steff fumbled in the chest of drawers for the thermometer. — Here we are.

Fran opened her mouth like a baby bird. Outside in the darkness the owl called again. Steff told it to shut up. She took Fran's temperature, pronounced it high, but not lethal, and gave her two Paracetamol.

— You know what they say, said Fran. — Have to be careful, immune system all haywire —

— Do you want me to call the hospital?

— No. I'll be okay.

— We shouldn't have gone out. You should have been sitting in the sun in the garden, just that for a bit.

— I wanted to go. It's just — could I have a hot water bottle?

— You could. Steff brought it, tucked it in, settled herself in the chair, and pulled the rug around her. — I'll stay until you're asleep.

— Angel.

Steff grunted. Fran closed her eyes and let warmth and comfort take her: away from the ceaseless rise and fall of her thoughts, away from the certainty that death was not far off, away from the swift gleam which seemed always to follow it, like a runner who would not give up, who brought news from elsewhere, waving a flag and calling: You can come through!

All that. All that. She yawned, as the shivering subsided, felt herself enter the beginning of a dream — just floating bits of this and that, nothing she would remember—and drifted back into sleep.

Next morning, Steff left her, so deeply comfortable, and went stiffly downstairs. She drew back the curtains onto a dewy day, gave Perseus his breakfast, made tea, yawning, heard the paper fall on to the mat, and the delivery man drive away. All this good everyday stuff: putting the things on the tea tray, glancing at the headlines—but how stiff and tired and bleak she was, after the broken night.

She climbed the stairs with a heavy heart. — Little sister mine, she heard herself say aloud, as a mug chinked against the pot. Then, on the landing, she called out brightly: — Here we are!

She came to the open bedroom door, and stopped on the threshold, knowing at once that something was different, something had changed, and in the quiet and stillness was just in time to hear Fran murmur— Kiss me, before she slipped away.

Acknowledgements

'Pegwell Day' was joint winner of the London Writers Competition in 1982. 'Back' was one of the winners of the first London Short Story Competition launched by the London Arts Board and the South Bank Centre in 1992. It was published in *Smoke Signals* by Serpent's Tail (1993) and is being recorded as part of National Short Story Week 2011. A different version of 'In Bratislava' was published by *You* magazine (*Mail on Sunday*) in 1996. 'Outside the House' was shortlisted for the 1995 London Writers Competition and broadcast on BBC Radio 4 in 1997, read by Eve Karpf. The version published here is altered in some details.

'Annunciation' was commissioned by BBC Radio 4 as part of their *Borderlands* series, and was broadcast in 2005, read by Stella Gonet. It was inspired by a painting of the same name (1968) by John Shelley, shown in the Tate Britain exhibition, *The Art of the Garden*, in 2004. 'Landscape at Iden' was inspired by another work in this exhibition, *Gunhills, Windley*, (1946-52) by Douglas Percy Bliss, as well as by the eponymous painting (1929) by Paul Nash. 'Five People Waiting' was first published in *You* magazine (*Mail on Sunday*) in 2007. 'Mother Duck' is based on a story told to me by Elizabeth Mackay.